Praise for
A WORLD BELOW

— — — — — — — — — —

"A swift-paced survival tale that's a cool blend of *Lord of the Flies* and *Journey to the Center of the Earth*."
— *School Library Journal*

"This richly imaginative field trip gone bad or amazing—depending on how you look at it—is a sharp meditation on the seemingly universal difficulties of being young, smart, and uncertain."
— *BCCB*

"The quick-paced adventure and positive message of setting aside past hurts are sure to appeal. A multi-faceted journey from darkness to light."
— *Kirkus Reviews*

— — — — — — —

A
WORLD
BELOW

WESLEY KING

A Paula Wiseman Book
Simon & Schuster Books for Young Readers
New York   London   Toronto   Sydney   New Delhi

SIMON & SCHUSTER BOOKS FOR YOUNG READERS

An imprint of Simon & Schuster Children's Publishing Division

1230 Avenue of the Americas, New York, New York 10020

This book is a work of fiction. Any references to historical events, real people, or real places are used
fictitiously. Other names, characters, places, and events are products of the author's imagination, and
any resemblance to actual events or places or persons, living or dead, is entirely coincidental.

Text copyright © 2018 by Wesley King

Cover illustrations copyright © 2018 by Nancy Liang

SIMON & SCHUSTER BOOKS FOR YOUNG READERS is a trademark of Simon & Schuster, Inc.

For information about special discounts for bulk purchases, please contact Simon & Schuster Special

Sales at 1-866-506-1949 or business@simonandschuster.com.

The Simon & Schuster Speakers Bureau can bring authors to your live event.

For more information or to book an event, contact the Simon & Schuster Speakers Bureau

at 1-866-248-3049 or visit our website at www.simonspeakers.com.

Also available in a Simon & Schuster Books for Young Readers hardcover edition

Interior design by Tom Daly

Cover design by Lucy Ruth Cummins

The text for this book was set in Weiss Std.

Manufactured in the United States of America

0719 OFF

First Simon & Schuster Books for Young Readers paperback edition August 2019

2 4 6 8 10 9 7 5 3 1

The Library of Congress has cataloged the hardcover edition as follows:

Names: King, Wesley, author.

Title: A world below / Wesley King.

Description: First Edition. | New York : Simon & Schuster Books for Young Readers, 2018. |
"A Paula Wiseman Book." | Summary: Mr. Baker's eighth grade class thought they were in for a
normal field trip to Carlsbad Caverns in New Mexico, but their journey takes a terrifying
turn when an earthquake hits and the students are plunged into a frigid underground
lake, forcing them to fight for survival and find their way back above ground.

Identifiers: LCCN 2017015619 | ISBN 9781481478229 (hardback) | ISBN 9781481478236 (pbk) |
ISBN 9781481478243 (eBook)

Subjects: | CYAC: School field trips—Fiction. | Earthquakes—Fiction. | Survival—Fiction. | Carlsbad
Caverns (N.M.)—Fiction. | BISAC: JUVENILE FICTION / Action & Adventure / Survival Stories. |
JUVENILE FICTION / Science Fiction. | JUVENILE FICTION / Mysteries & Detective Stories.

Classification: LCC PZ7.K58922 Wo 2018 | DDC [Fic]—dc23

LC record available at https://lccn.loc.gov/2017015619

For Juliana, who gives me a reason to come back to the real world
(and never complains when I wander off again)

A
WORLD
BELOW

Edgewood Middle School | 05/06/17
Mr. Baker's Class | Carlsbad Caverns Field Trip
Parent Supervisor: Ms. Johnson

Greg Alvarez

Joanne Bennett

Eric Johnson

Derek Jones

Naj Kahn

Ashley Lewski

Brian Little

Tom Pike

Mary Robinson

Marta Robinson

Silvia Rodrigues

Leonard Tam

Shannon Woods

Jordan Zanowitz

Consider everyone on this list as missing or deceased. Notify parents immediately. Pictures for identification of bodies may be required.
    —Officer Daniel Brown

Twenty Minutes Before

THE BOY SAT ON A THRONE MADE OF MUSHROOM stalks and branches, slung together in an arching, triangular shape and lashed tight with vines. Thorns and brambles had been missed in the soldiers' haste, and now they dug into his legs and back, pinching and twisting and sharp.

But the boy did not flinch. He was as motionless as the throne he sat upon.

The boy had dark hair that spilled down his face in dry, knotted clumps, reaching his shoulders. He was thin but muscular, with the narrow jaw of a thirteen-year-old protruding below pale, thin lips and black eyes. He was still considered a boy, even there in the unforgiving dark. But this boy was the King, and there was a judgment to be made.

His soldiers brought the offender before him, dragging the frantic child by two skinny arms. The edge of the Ghost Woods stood behind the King, the towering white and crimson fungi and gnarled barbar trees watched the scene impassively. The chamber was deathly still.

The offender was even younger than the King—as pale as the mushrooms and stained with dirt and fresh blood from a cut above his right eyebrow. His hair was long and unruly as well, hanging down past his shoulders and tangled with snake vines— it looked as if they might have grown from his skull. He was ten or eleven years old, but his eyes were hard and seething with hatred. The sight of them made the King stir.

"The Worm," Captain Salez said solemnly, taking up his post beside the King.

"What is his crime?" the King murmured.

The King clasped his trembling hands in his lap to still them.

The haphazard throne had been built on the border of the woods just an hour earlier by his men. They had been hunting for a Night Rat when the cries had gone up: A Worm had been found hunting on the King's Land. The King knew the crime. He also knew the punishment.

But there were formalities to follow. All offenders were to be tried by the King.

Captain Salez straightened. "This Worm was discovered skinning a freshly dead Night Rat on your land, my King. The boy's spear was still lodged in its torso when discovered. The Worm then tried to flee and harmed one of your soldiers in the process."

The King nodded slowly. He wished his father were here, but he was long dead now. Sometimes he imagined that his father was sitting beside him, hard as stone, passing judgment. The boy knew what his words would be: *The Law is paramount. It must be death.*

"Do you have anything to say in your defense, Worm?" the boy King asked.

The young Worm looked up at him, his lip twisting. "I have committed no crime."

He was thin, but wiry and strong for his age. He would have been a good soldier.

"You have heard the charges," the King said, frowning at the boy's impertinence.

"I heard them," he spat. "But Jana says your land is ours too. So . . . I did nothing wrong."

The King's attending soldiers—twenty strong and armed with sword and spear and jagged knife—stiffened at the comment. The boy shouldn't have mentioned Jana. There was no name more hated in the entire Midnight Realm than hers—the one who had plunged them into war and who now called herself the Shadow Queen, a blatant challenge to the King.

The boy would suffer now, if his soldiers had their way.

The King studied the Worm thoughtfully. The boys' ribs were visible above a roughly sewn loincloth of rat hide and yew leaves. His gaunt cheeks seemed sickly and alien, buried beneath grime, and yet he looked much the same as the King and his soldiers. Of course he did.

"What is your name?" the King asked.

"Nennez," he replied proudly.

"Are you alone?"

"Yes," he replied, looking offended. "I need no help to hunt."

"Do you know the sentence for trespassing on the King's Land?" the King asked.

The boy finally turned his proud eyes down. His knees were shaking now. "Yes."

The King sat back in his throne, feeling the jagged thorns poking into his flesh. It was an easy decision, in truth, but it didn't feel like one. Nennez looked like the younger brother he had never had—they might have grown up together in the Hall, stalking roaches. He had done nothing wrong but try to feed himself. Did he truly deserve death?

"The Law is clear," Captain Salez said, as if sensing the King's doubts.

The King just stared at Nennez. "If you were spared, what would you do?"

The soldiers all looked at their King, uncomprehending.

Nennez seemed equally stunned. "I . . . I would go back to my people."

"Will you stay off my land?" the King asked softly.

The boy's bottom lip was moving now, quivering like a fish on the line. "Yes."

The King paused. It was unfathomable to let a Worm go for trespassing. But he was already tired of passing death on Worms. Two had gone to death on his orders.

"Go. Tell Jana to keep your people away. And try to be—"

He didn't get a chance to finish. Suddenly the Earth shook like a writhing animal in a net, casting the King from his throne. The cave came alive with screams and panic as the sound of cracking, splintering stone filled the air. Nennez took off in a flash, using the panic to his advantage, and the King felt Captain Salez's strong hands heaving him to his feet.

"Get back to the village!" Captain Salez shouted, waving at the other soldiers.

Captain Salez dragged the King toward the tunnels, shielding the boy's head from the falling rocks. The last thing the King saw was Nennez vanish into the darkness, and he wondered if the Mother had decided to punish them all for his mercy.

He could almost see his father walking behind him now, a cold expression on his face. *Weakness will be punished*, he said sharply. *There can be no weak Midnight King.*

Captain Salez pulled the King back into the tunnel, and his father disappeared.

I am sorry, Father. I will be strong. I will not break the Law again.

One Month Before

ERIC WAS JUST DOZING OFF WHEN MR. BAKER skipped into the class. He barely managed to open his eyes, and felt a little saliva pooling on his bottom lip. Eric wiped it, hoping no one had noticed.

Eric usually didn't reach full consciousness until at least noon—and that was on a good day. Every morning he dragged himself out of bed like a marionette with half the strings cut, ate a bowl of Cocoa Puffs because it at least gave him a little sugar rush, and then shuffled onto the crowded town bus, his sleep-fogged eyes fixed on one foot after the other and nothing else. Just that morning he had walked into a light pole outside his house—he had the bruise to prove it. Though, in fairness, it was tough to get up when there was no one to yell at you.

His mother worked early at a local café as a server, so the house was always empty in the morning. Apart from Patterson Pawmaster, of course, but a twenty-year-old Border Collie probably didn't count. He didn't even bark anymore. He was like a geriatric Lassie. Still, Patterson at least waited for an ear scratch from his familiar perch atop the living room couch. He was probably the only one who would notice if Eric just stayed in bed.

Eric didn't have any friends, or any close ones, at least. He occasionally talked to Dan Piller at recess, an equally reclusive kid in his class who loved exchanging sarcastic banter, but that was about it. Eric kind of liked it—being alone. It was safer that way.

Eric glanced up at Mr. Baker just as he pivoted sharply in front of the Smart Board. Mr. Baker nodded his head in greeting, his eyes pausing for just a moment on the disheveled Eric.

"Morning, class," Mr. Baker said cheerily, clapping two fleshy pink hands together.

Mr. Baker was always cheery. He often dressed in checkered cardigans—red and blue, usually—wore oversize, almost cartoonish bow ties, and had a pair of thick-framed black glasses that sat perched atop his very large nose. He was constantly touching and adjusting them as he looked around, as if they were a set of binoculars that he used to zoom in on his students.

"Morning, Mr. Baker," a few students replied.

The Keeners, as Eric called them. They sat at the front of the class and seemed to genuinely love school, which was annoying first thing in the morning. They were all supposed to love school, technically, seeing how this was the advanced class, but the Keeners took that to heart more than the rest of them. Joanne, Shannon, the twins—Marta and Mary, who basically never separated—Naj, and Brian were the main ones. Eric could have joined the Keeners, maybe. His grades were right at the top of the class, and he did sort of like school, other than the early start time. But Eric wasn't one for answering questions or participating. He liked his isolated corner near the back, tucked beside a bookshelf stacked with dusty old math textbooks. Everyone ignored that corner, and Eric along with it.

"I have some news," Mr. Baker said, still smiling.

The Keeners looked attentive. No one else did. Tom Pike was talking in the corner.

"About the graduation trip," Mr. Baker continued meaningfully.

That got their attention. Eric saw Silvia Rodrigues perk up at the far side of the class, brushing her hair aside and focusing on Mr. Baker for the first time since he had walked into the class. Silvia was . . . well . . . Eric's favorite person. She was a great writer and the best in the class at biology, particularly botany and zoology, and she was also a star long-distance runner. Not to mention she had the biggest green eyes he had ever seen. Eric spent at least half his day stealing glances at her when she wasn't looking.

Mr. Baker hurried over to his computer, letting the silence hang.

"Go on . . . ," Tom Pike said, eliciting a few laughs.

That was Tom. He was the hockey team captain and looked the part: always wearing his brown leather team jacket, and with matching hair cropped short like a soldier's. But they didn't have stereotypical jocks in the advanced class—everyone here had to excel in academics, after all. Tom was particularly good at drama and music and almost always got the lead roles. Eric was usually a stagehand. Tom was apparently a gifted mathlete as well, though Eric never went to watch the competitions. Math was his least favorite subject by far, and he refused, on principle, to ever call anyone a mathlete.

Two of Tom's teammates, both in hockey and mathletes, were in the class too—Derek and Leonard—and they both followed him around everywhere, snickering and telling idiotic jokes. It was kind of sickening, really. Except their jokes switched between hockey and mathematical references, like, "Dude, that guy skates slower than you solve for x." Even the cool kids in advanced classes were kind of weird.

Mr. Baker emphatically clicked something on his laptop and then stood up again, grinning from ear to ear as an image appeared on the Smart Board. He turned to it, beaming.

Eric frowned. It was a picture of a cave—some stalactites and a bat.

"What is that?" Silvia asked, sounding concerned.

"*That* is Carlsbad Caverns," Mr. Baker said proudly. "One of the most intricate and amazing cave systems on Earth. And I, your Mr. Baker, have just gotten permission to take you all there."

A few people exchanged looks. Eric just sighed and put his head in his hands.

"Yes, Silvia?" Mr. Baker asked.

"Last year they got to spend two nights in Albuquerque. They got to go see a play and eat at La Friche and then they got to stay in a nice hotel with a pool and stuff."

Eric glanced up to see Mr. Baker adjust his glasses, as if to zoom in a bit more.

"So?" Mr. Baker asked, frowning.

Silvia looked flustered. "So . . . I thought that was what we were going to do."

Mr. Baker laughed and turned to the Smart Board. "We're going to Carlsbad Caverns, Silvia! The home of the Big Room . . . the largest chamber in North America! Do you even understand how big that cave is going to be? You're going to love it. Trust me, Albuquerque has nothing on this. I'll have permission forms at the end of the day. Twenty bucks for the bus! That's it. Last year they had to pay two hundred. Ha! Crazy. In honor of this exciting news, we're going to start today with a little geology. Who can tell me about limestone? Anyone?"

Eric looked up to see Silvia exchange a horrified look with her best friend, Ashley Lewski, and then he just smiled and put his head down again. They were going to a cave. Super.

One month later, Eric woke up to a face in the dark. It was the first time in at least three years.

"Up we get," his mother said, her curly hair already pulled back into a bun.

Eric just stared up at her, confused. His stomach felt like an old loaf of bread.

"What . . . time?" he croaked.

"Five in the morning," she replied cheerily. "We have to be at the school at five-thirty!"

"This is too early to be alive."

She scoffed and threw the blanket off him. Cold rushed in greedily underneath.

"Nonsense! This is a sleep-in! Now get your skinny butt out of bed."

With that she rushed out of the room, and Eric just lay there covered in goose bumps and wondering why he had ever told his mother about this field trip. He had never expected her to actually volunteer as chaperone. It was basically his worst nightmare. Finally, he swung his legs out of bed, shivering. His room was littered with books—they lined the shelves and covered his desk and were strewn haphazardly about the floor. He kept his favorites on his nightstand in case he ever wanted to read something familiar before bed, number one being *My Side of the Mountain* by Jean Craighead George. He had read that book a hundred times at least; it was about a boy named Sam Gribley who left his family's apartment in New York City and set off to live by himself in the woods. Eric had thought about running away plenty of times, and he knew just about every trick for surviving in the wild. But when he told his mom about his big plans, she said she would track him down and he would be very, *very* sorry. As a result, he hadn't quite mustered the courage to go. Yet.

Yawning, Eric made his way to the bathroom, wiping the sleep from his eyes.

"Do you want breakfast?" his mom called upstairs.

"Nothing could sound less appetizing," he replied miserably.

He stared at himself in the mirror. He *was* skinny—enough

that his ribs and collarbone were clearly visible. He had his mother's thick black hair and full lips, but his dad's pointed nose and blue eyes. His skin was a light brown as a result of both parents— they called him *biracial* at his mom's work once, and just *mixed* at school when he was younger. Both sounded kind of weird. He didn't feel mixed. He just felt like himself.

He brushed his teeth and tried to tame his always tousled hair—a losing battle—and then went to throw on some clothes. Mr. Baker said it was cool in the caves, so he put on some jeans and a T-shirt. He went to grab a windbreaker, along with a flashlight and a few other supplies that Mr. Baker had listed, but his mom had grabbed all that and already had it packed up by the front door. She seemed oddly excited to go on the field trip. He told her that made one of them.

Ten minutes later they were on their way to the school.

"So, I look forward to meeting some of your classmates," she said. "Especially Silvia."

Eric sighed. "Please don't look, speak, or even gesture at her today. Then it's going to be obvious that I mentioned her to you, which, by the way, I regret."

"You are too dramatic."

"I am pleasantly invisible at school," he reminded her. "I don't want that to change."

"Why not?"

"Because there are worse things than autonomy," he said.

She snorted. "Sometimes you talk like a forty-year-old. Where did you get that from?"

"*Dr. Who*, probably," he said. "But I'm serious. No referring to her . . . ever. Please."

"Fine," she said. "But you are twelve now. Sometimes feelings of infatuation can start—"

"Please no."

She laughed, and then glanced at him. "There is something else I wanted to mention."

"Is it about the birds and the bees? Because I'm going to tuck and roll if so."

"Well . . . technically. I was asked out on a date last night. I would like to go."

Eric turned to her, frowning. "First of all . . . gross. Second of all . . . by who? When? How?"

"Thanks for the vote of confidence," she muttered. "A patron at the café. His name is Frank. He is very nice. And I said I would think about it, but I took his number. It's time, Eric."

His dad had left three years ago now. He had a new family in Phoenix, apparently, including Eric's half sister. He had only talked to his dad one time since then, on his tenth birthday. He had called for, like, two minutes to say happy birthday and Eric had said a few mean things that he kind of but not really regretted later. That had been the end of their relationship.

"Well . . . as long as I never have to hear anything about it," Eric said slowly. "Ever."

"Deal. Ah, we're here."

She pulled into the school parking lot, where a yellow school bus was already parked and waiting. Mr. Baker was standing at the open door, looking absolutely and expectedly ridiculous in an explorer's cap and matching leather satchel over one shoulder, along with some beige cargo pants hiked way up with suspenders and knee-high black rubber boots. He looked he was setting out to look for King Kong in the new world. Eric sighed deeply.

"So that's Mr. Baker," his mom said. "He looks fun."

"That's one word for him," Eric said.

Soon Eric was sitting on the bus, curled up against the window watching one student after another get dropped off. They glanced at him as they got on and kept walking, finding seats near the back, which was apparently cool despite Eric's longstanding belief that convenience was cooler. Tom was the last one to arrive—his dad looking like a retired quarterback—and when he sat down, Eric's mom and Mr. Baker climbed onboard.

Eric's mom plopped down next to Eric, and he thought he heard snickers behind him.

This is going to be lots of fun, Eric thought miserably.

Mr. Baker stood at the front of the bus and saluted. "Greetings, explorers of the deep!"

A couple of people replied with, "Morning." More looked like they were still asleep.

"I bet you have noticed by now that there is no bus driver . . . surprise! I got my license." He held the card up, grinning. "This is going to be great. Hopefully, you have all packed according to my instructions. Just a snack, of course. We will be stopping at a fast food place on the way home. I hope you brought lots of water. Now, attendance!"

He began scrolling down the list, receiving half-hearted responses and sighs.

"Eric Johnson?"

"He's here!" his mother volunteered.

"Thank you, Mrs. Johnson," Mr. Baker said, smiling and writing the name down.

"Just a Ms. now," she replied, and there were more snickers.

Eric sank lower into his seat as the attendance continued.

"Silvia Rodrigues?" he called.

"Here," someone groaned at the back.

Eric's mom went to turn around, and he quickly grabbed her arm. "Remember . . ."

"Right," she said, winking. "Your secret is safe with me."

Eric tried to find a way to slink down even lower, but his legs were pinned. She was never going to make it through an entire day without blowing his cover.

When he was finished, Mr. Baker put the sheet down, clapped his hands, and climbed into the driver's seat. "All aboard! We are off to one of the world's natural wonders. Just three hours to go! It will fly by. I have some songs, of course, but perhaps we can start with a little summary of what we want to see! Who wants to go first?"

Silence.

"I'll start," he said, unabashed. "I have heard wonderful things about the Mystery—"

"Wake me when we get there," Eric muttered. "Or better yet, after the trip is over."

The bus rumbled out of the parking lot, first jerking to a start and then jumping right over the curb onto the street. Eric's head smacked into the window with a pronounced *thud*.

"Ha!" Mr. Baker shouted. "My apologies, class. Never fear, though! One little bump, but I am sure the rest of this trip will be smooth sailing! Carlsbad Caverns, here we come! Mush!"

Eric rubbed his head, scowling.

Two Hours Before

SILVIA STEPPED OFF THE BUS AND WAS GREETED by a blast of dry desert wind. It seemed to be carting half the sand in the area with it, and she groaned as she turned away and tried to cover her eyes.

Silvia was already miserable.

They'd hit at least ten curbs on the three-hour bus ride. Every time, Mr. Baker shouted, "Last one!" and then laughed uproariously like a maniacal pirate captain. To make matters worse, her best friend, Ashley, had decided to talk the entire way, mostly about boys, so Silvia hadn't gotten even a minute of sleep. She was exhausted.

She didn't sleep much as it was, even on a normal night, so waking up at four-thirty was definitely not helping. She could feel the fatigue sitting in her bones and at the fringes of her mind, like little bursts of static electricity that flared without warning. Silvia was always more vulnerable when she was tired.

She would have to stay focused and calm until she got home.

As the rest of the class filed out of the bus, Mr. Baker hurried to the front, looking ridiculous with his cap and man purse. It had been a month now since he first announced the trip, and he had been talking about it every day since like it was the greatest thing to ever happen to any of them. They had covered the entire geological make-up of the caverns, the subterranean flora and fauna that lived there, and the map of the known sections about a hundred times. Silvia had even had to draw her own version of the map, with labels and dates of discovery. Mr. Baker said he was going to save the history of who had discovered the caves for their visit . . . thrilling. Silvia was already sick of the caverns.

Two weeks ago, Mr. Baker sent every student home with a list that had been stained a blotchy yellow with tea, like they were early treasure hunters.

We are soon embarking on a trip into Carlsbad Caverns . . . the doorway to the center of the Earth! Who knows what we will find down there in the darkness? At the very least, one of the most fascinating geological spots in the entire state. Maybe the country.

Wow!

Now, to prepare for this adventure, you will need to bring the following:

Two bottles of water. We will be doing lots of walking!

Breakfast for the bus and a light snack! We will have lunch there and stop for fast food on the way home.

A flashlight! A true explorer always brings a flashlight.

Comfortable shoes for walking!

An intrepid spirit and a thirst to explore the unknown and wonderful!
If you have any questions, feel free to ask me. It's going to be AWESOME.

Even her mom had laughed at the note. But Silvia had brought what he said, other than the intrepid spirit maybe. Her dad had been as excited about the trip as Mr. Baker, though, and had even added a Swiss Army knife to her backpack. When she asked what exactly she was supposed to do with a Swiss Army knife in the caves, he had replied, "You never know! That's why they have so many tools on there, Silvia. Better safe than sorry." She had just groaned and walked away.

To be fair, she was interested in the science of the place. Silvia was particularly fascinated with biology, and it would be cool if she could find some troglodytic creatures down there that she could examine. The problem was that she didn't love the idea of walking around with a thousand feet of solid rock over her head. She wasn't *technically* claustrophobic . . . but close.

"Welcome!" Mr. Baker said happily. "Not a bad drive at all, right?"

There was no comment from the group. Someone grumbled. He didn't seem to notice.

"Now, we are all prepaid and signed up, so we can go right in. They offered us a guide, but naturally I think I can handle that. I have read three books on the caverns in the last month."

"You need a girlfriend, Mr. Baker," Tom remarked.

Everyone laughed.

"Piddle posh," he said. "Time spent reading is never wasted."

He turned and gestured to the visitor center—a squat, sandstone building where a few people were snapping pictures and posing. There were two entrances to Carlsbad Caverns: the natural entrance—a broad, shadowy opening that was surrounded by a manmade amphitheater and connected to the Bat Cave—and the elevator shaft that plunged directly downward from the visitor center. Mr. Baker had loudly and endlessly debated, but decided the elevator shaft was a better bet for their limited time, as it would take them right to the center of the caves. From there they were going to explore the Big Room and then make their way down to the Queen's Chamber. They had five hours to make it through.

Silvia saw that Jordan had brought an old fold-out map of the caverns and was looking at it eagerly.

"We are off to explore a world long forgotten by the sun," Mr. Baker began. "We will see wonders of geology that you will never forget, dating back millions of years into the deep, dark past, and if we're lucky, some underground creatures as well. Remember what I said: At last count, there are some four hundred thousand bats living in the caverns. Can you even imagine that many bats?"

Ashley groaned. "This just keeps getting better."

"I agree," Mr. Baker said cheerfully. "Follow me!"

He turned and hurried off, and Silvia exchanged a resigned look with Ashley. Ashley had been her best friend since kindergarten, and they were rarely apart for long. She looked about as different from Silvia as possible—curly blond hair, tons of freckles, and a big, crooked grin—and their personalities were just as opposite. Ashley was bubbly, outgoing, and loved to gossip, whereas Silvia was a bit more withdrawn and quiet. There were some good reasons for that, of course, but she didn't share those with anyone but her parents. Mostly just her mom, actually.

Ashley also liked to pretend she was dumb, even though she worked hard and aced every test. This was a source of constant frustration for Silvia, who told her she should be proud of her grades, but Ashley said she didn't want to be labeled a nerd. Her older sister, Tabitha, was very popular and *very* vain, and Ashley idolized her.

"This is going to be a long day," Ashley muttered, looking around the desert. A few cacti stared back, sticking out among the sun-weathered boulders. They were just about the only break from the endless sand and stone. "Maybe there will be some cute boys down there."

"In a cave?" Silvia said, rolling her eyes.

"You never know."

"You have issues," Silvia said, and Ashley just laughed.

They followed the rest of the class into the visitor center. Eric and his mom were right behind them, Eric's eyes locked firmly on his shuffling feet. Silvia had never seen anyone more reclusive in her entire life. He never seemed interested in talking to anybody. She knew he was brilliant—she had snuck a few peeks at his test grades—but she always wondered why he seemed so reluctant to make friends or participate in the class. Sometimes he looked just plain miserable.

He looked even more forlorn today, probably because his mom was with him. She had sat down right next to Eric on the bus, eliciting some laughs from Derek and Leonard, and a none-too-quiet quip of "mama's boy" that Eric must have heard. They were both jerks, really.

"Derek looks cute today, don't you think?" Ashley said, eyeing the boys in front of them.

Tom, Derek, and Leonard were laughing among themselves, walking just ahead. All three were wearing beige shorts, sneakers, and different colored golf shirts: red, blue, and yellow. Even their haircuts were similar: short and gelled to look like it was naturally spiky.

"He looks the same as yesterday. And every other day. They must call each other to plan their outfits ahead, honestly."

"He has a new shirt today. I haven't seen him in yellow."

Silvia sighed. "Why don't you just tell him you like him?"

Ashley looked at her, horrified. "Because he would laugh at me."

"Who says?"

"I do. Don't mention it again or I'll throw you down a hole."

"You'll have plenty of options," Silvia muttered.

Mr. Baker ushered the students into the elevator, saluting as they passed as if they were going into battle. She saw Jordan stop and snap a picture of the elevator doors on his cell phone—*he* seemed excited for the caves, at least. He was a big, burly kid with a mop of bright red hair and a lot of freckles. He usually just hung out with his best friend, Greg, a mousy kid with a mushroom cut and glasses who was a big-time history buff. Jordan checked his picture and then scurried into the elevator. Silvia looked out the nearest window one last time, suddenly hesitant to get into the elevator. The desert sky was clear, apart from a few lazy clouds drifting past overhead like cotton balls. It was a beautiful day.

"Goodbye, sky," she said sarcastically.

Ashley laughed, and then they followed the others into the elevator. The doors slid shut and Silvia looked around uneasily. It was a little bit tight in there. Someone pressed the button.

"Next stop . . . a boring field trip," Tom muttered.

Then the elevator plunged into the Earth.

"The Big Room," Mr. Baker said dramatically, leading them into the massive chamber.

They had been studying the geological formations in the Big Room for three weeks now, but seeing it in person was staggering. The vaulted cavern ceiling stretched far overhead, covered with limestone formations and stalactites that loomed over them like the teeth of some monolithic beast. Lights had been strategically placed throughout the Big Room to illuminate the chamber, casting a stark white glare on certain sections while creating fluid shadows that seemed to shift with every step.

They passed the towering Rock of Ages and the Temple of the Sun, famous rock columns that dwarfed the others, rising up like Aztec pyramids. The class seemed to grow smaller and smaller as they walked into the middle of the Big Room along the weaving pathway, which was marked with steel railings and signs. Their voices echoed around them, growing softer and softer and then vanishing. Even Ashley fell silent as she stared up at a beautiful white column.

"Okay, this is decent," she finally whispered.

"It was a boy who first documented this," Mr. Baker said from the front. "Jim White. A cowboy if there ever was one, and a true adventurer. He came upon these caves while searching for lost cattle and said that he first spotted a great plume of black bats, which he thought might be a whirlwind or a volcano. Upon investigating, he found a great hole, and knew that there must be a massive place down there to house so many bats. He came back a few days later with nothing but a hatchet, some rope, and a lantern, and he began to explore. He found the Bat Cave, among other amazing caverns, and had a great fright when his lantern went out. Jim said, 'It seemed as though a million tons of black wool descended upon me.' You can imagine his terror."

Silvia thought about being stuck down here without a light, and shivered.

"Luckily he had more kerosene, and he made it out again. He returned soon after with a fifteen-year-old Mexican boy whose name is now lost, though in his book Jim White called him the Kid or Muchacho. Jim White went on to tell his story in a booklet called *Jim White's Own Story* and became somewhat famous, while no one really knows what happened to the Kid."

Mr. Baker suddenly smiled and pulled an old book out of his satchel, thin and yellowed.

"And I've been reading it, as you can see! This rare copy of *Jim White's Own Story* will go as a prize to whomever answers a trivia question on the way home . . . so try and take mental notes. I haven't decided on the question just yet. But back to the Kid.

Some say he disappeared from the face of the Earth, but in all likelihood, he just returned to his village, and he was never really included in the fanfare that followed the release of Jim White's book. I wonder if the Kid ever knew how famous their story became. Do his ancestors even know it was him?"

He gestured around the enormous cavern.

"Astounding, really. Can you imagine being the first to walk these caves? To enter this alien world? What an adventure that must have been. Who knows? Maybe we'll discover some new parts ourselves."

He skipped on ahead, and the class followed him, their heads swiveling to take in the spectacular scenery. Silvia stared up at the great stalactites looming over them, wondering if any had ever fallen before. Some looked to be at least ten feet long and were massive at their conical bases. They probably each weighed several tons. Feeling her skin prickle at the thought, she quickly started after the others, sticking close to Ashley. As they walked, she glanced back again at Eric, who followed the class about ten yards behind, moving as silently as a ghost. He was looking up at the cavern ceiling though, and even he seemed a little impressed.

His mom was sticking right by his side, reading a brochure and pointing as they walked.

"This is simply amazing," she said. "Did you know that this is the largest—"

"I literally know everything about these caves," Eric said, cutting her off.

She snorted. "Is that so?"

"Trust me. I could write *Eric Johnson's Own Story* on this after we leave."

"Frank said we just *have* to see the Queen's Chamber."

"Frank the guy you met for, like, five minutes at the diner?"

"I told him I was coming here. He's really nice. He's a commercial pilot—"

"I thought we agreed never to talk about Frank."

She sighed. "Well, I thought you would change your mind. . . ."

"I'm moving into the caves. That's it."

"Don't be a smarty-pants."

"Did you actually just say that?" Eric said. "Are you, like, ninety all of a sudden?"

Silvia bit back a laugh. She had never heard Eric speak that much. Ever.

"You know, Mr. Baker is cute . . . in a nerdy kind of way."

"Please stop."

"Think he's single?"

"I'm going to find a hole to jump into," Eric said.

"Maybe I should ask . . ."

This time Silvia snorted with laughter, unable to hold it in, and Eric stopped talking immediately. He and his mom dropped back from the group a little more, and Ashley and Silvia just exchanged an amused look and kept walking.

"Mr. Talkative all of a sudden," Ashley whispered. "What a weirdo."

Silvia didn't reply.

As another few hours rolled by, Silvia began to yearn to leave the caves. They had already looped back and explored the Queen's Chamber, which had been beautiful, with its pure limestone columns and natural arches. But still, she was starting to get sick of the stuffy underground air and the hard, unforgiving rock beneath her sneakers. The whole place made her wish for clear, open skies or her bedroom and a comfortable couch.

"My feet hurt," Ashley said.

"Same."

Silvia had a track meet next week, and she didn't want to *start* with sore feet.

Mr. Baker was leading them down a narrow passage, his flashlight bobbing ahead of them, landing on every spot of quartz or nook or cranny. Silvia could hear him cheerfully explaining how Jim White and the Kid had walked in this very spot, lighting their way with a flickering kerosene lamp. She shined her own flashlight along the walls, illuminating cracks and crevices and scattered holes by the thousands. She wondered if any bats were hiding in there. She kind of hoped she would spot one, but she knew it was unlikely they would live down in this end of the cave where there were no easy exits to the outside. Cave-dwelling bats had to leave to find bugs or fruits or nectar, depending on the species, and there were none of those necessities down here in the dark. In fact, she hadn't seen a single animal yet, which was disappointing.

"Think we're done soon?" Silvia asked hopefully.

Ashley snorted. "I doubt it. Mr. Baker could probably spend all week down here. But we have to leave in a couple of hours. We're supposed to be home at eight, and we still have to stop to eat."

The passage they were in was only about ten feet high and the same across, and it was small enough that Silvia was starting to feel uncomfortable. The little tingling at the edge of her mind was back again, and she felt the familiar uneasy feeling settling into her stomach. She pictured the walls cracking and the ceiling raining down.

Just relax, she told herself. *This would not be a good place to freak out.*

"You all right?" Ashley asked, looking at her in concern. "You look nervous."

"Fine. Just ready to get out of here."

"Agreed," Ashley muttered. "Let's go talk to Mr. Baker."

Ahead, the class had emerged into another chamber. Mr. Baker was checking his guide book and analyzing the ceiling and rock formations, mumbling to himself through a wide grin.

"Mr. Baker?" Eric's mom said, her voice echoing around the chamber.

He looked up. "Yes, Ms. Johnson?"

"I realized I left a few snacks for the group on the bus. Totally forgot them. I was going to go grab them now and set them up in the lunch room for when we head back that way. You mind? Figured have some watermelon and orange slices with lunch to get our strength back."

"Sounds perfect! We will be here for a little while, not to worry."

"Great," she said. She gave Eric a pat on the shoulder. "Be back soon, sweetie."

He flushed redder than a fire hydrant and quickly turned away. Derek snickered.

As Ms. Johnson hurried off, Mr. Baker suddenly gasped and held a finger to his mouth.

"Shh," he said, lowering his voice. "This is the Mystery Room . . . so named for an unexplained noise that occurs only here. No one knows what it is. It could be wind from far away, or perhaps running water behind the walls. Some even say it's the ghosts of Jim White and the Kid, wandering the caverns, looking for the way out again. Fascinating, really. Listen!"

Everyone fell silent. And then they heard it. Rumbling.

"Is that it?" Shannon asked.

Mr. Baker frowned. "I guess so. I read it was more like breathing."

The rumbling started to get louder, like an explosion echoing from far away.

And then the cavern started to shake.

Silvia gasped as the floor moved violently beneath her, causing her to stumble. The quiet was suddenly broken by screams. The shaking intensified, and everything started to move in a strange blur, like time had sped up and slowed down all at once. Silvia fell into the chamber wall, catching herself painfully and reaching out for Ashley, who hit the rock hard beside her, smacking her forehead. Dust and debris and rock fragments started to rain down from the ceiling in dense clouds. Mr. Baker waved his hands, trying to keep his balance.

"Stay calm!" he said. "Follow me! We're going to head back to the tunnel."

He started to make his way back when a massive *crack* split the air. Silvia grabbed Ashley's hand as the whole room shook violently around them. Brian, a quiet boy who sat at the front of class, was lying on the ground in front of them, holding his head where he had been hit by a falling rock and groaning. Ahead, even Mr. Baker froze at the sound of the loud crack. And then there was another.

Silvia looked down in horror. It was coming from underneath them.

"Run!" Mr. Baker yelled. "Come on!"

He ran to the back of the group, gesturing for them to follow, and then started for the tunnel. He never made it. The ground split open beneath him, and with a last shout, he was gone.

Terrified screams filled the cavern, mixed with sobs and shouts of "Mr. Baker!"

Silvia pulled a stunned Ashley forward, trying to escape the Mystery Room before it was swallowed up by the spreading rift in the floor.

"Watch out for the hole!" Tom shouted, heading around the edge. "Mr. Baker!"

The class started for the tunnel, with Eric, who had been far behind the others, now in the lead. He was white with fear as he tried to keep his footing and head after his mother. The class had almost made it into the tunnel when another horrendous crack erupted through the Mystery Room. Silvia stumbled forward and saw the ground violently wrench itself open like cracking ice, falling away beneath them.

She screamed, still holding Ashley's hand, and plummeted into the darkness.

The Fall

FOR A MOMENT, ERIC FELT AS IF HE WAS DREAMING. There were echoing screams and wild lights and a cold, enveloping darkness, but he was oddly calm. And then the water hit him like a truck.

The air rushed out of his mouth in a whoosh. He tried to shout, but water flooded down his throat. He could feel the freezing water like stabbing knives on every inch of his skin. Eric flailed desperately for the surface. It was so black that he couldn't even see his own grasping hands in front of him.

One thing was for sure: He was *moving*. A powerful current was whipping him along, causing him to spin and thrash and roll. He lashed out in all directions, desperate for air. Finally, he broke the roiling surface, gasping for oxygen. The air was full of pounding water, as loud as a hurricane, but above it, he could hear the screams.

"Help me!"

"What's happening?"

"Mr. Baker!"

The frantic words bounced off one another and jumbled together. Eric realized that the river was driving them away from the Mystery Room . . . and water never ran upward. The grim realization sunk in: They were being dragged deeper into the Earth. He fumbled blindly for his flashlight, but he must have dropped it.

His mind was spinning with fear. His arms were tiring from fighting the raging current. He coughed up more water. He knew he was in trouble. If his muscles cramped and tired, he would surely be killed.

Eric tried to focus. His body was still aching from the impact and the freezing cold water, but he couldn't panic now. He tried to think back to every survival story he had ever read. The hero always stayed calm and thought logically. *Slow down. Come up with a plan.* His brain stopped firing off its warning klaxons just long enough to think. He had to get out of the water.

The last thought finally connected. Something he could do.

He wasn't a great swimmer, but he at least knew where to aim: either side of the current that was relentlessly pulling him along. He pushed with everything he had, driving through the water and trying not to choke. Finally, his right hand connected with a rock *before* it slipped back into the water, and he clung to it, gripping its sharp edges with both hands and heaving himself forward until he was perched atop it like a coiled snake, unwilling to let go.

He heard more frantic screams as his classmates were dragged past him one after another.

"Swim for the sides!" he shouted. "Swim! I found the shore!"

"Eric!" a familiar voice replied, just audible over the rapids. It was Silvia. "Eric!"

"I'm here," he called, reaching out wildly with one hand to try and catch her. "Grab me!"

"Where are you?" Her voice was already growing fainter. "Eric!"

"Silvia!" he stretched out even farther, almost tumbling back into the water.

Her voice was gone. They sped past him in haunting, echoing waves: Tom, Naj, Joanne, Brian. Each time he shouted and tried to reach out to grab them, but he missed them all. Soon the shouts were only echoes at the edge of his hearing, and then they vanished down the river.

Eric lay on his rock, surrounded by pitch blackness and roaring water. He was alone.

For a minute or two he just stayed there, clinging to the freezing, slick surface of the rock and letting the river pound against his legs, too scared and stunned and cold to even think.

Get out of the water.

The thought struck again, and Eric snapped into action. Reaching blindly, he crawled onto solid ground, testing with his fingers. The water slipped away past his knees and then vanished altogether. He crawled onto a ledge, cold and slippery, and kept moving until he felt a wall. Then he huddled against that, drawing his legs in and hugging them to his chest, shivering violently. Eric tried to think. Should he go after the class? What if the river plunged into a hole farther down? What if it ran on forever until it emptied into some molten lake in the Earth's core?

No. He had to stay out of the water. Maybe he could find a way to follow them on land.

And to do that, he needed light.

His flashlight was gone, but he dug his cell phone out of his pocket and tried it, hopefully. His case, a gift from his mom last Christmas, was supposedly waterproof. But when he hit the power button, nothing happened.

"Come on," he pleaded, stripping the case off.

He took out the battery and put it back in, working only by feel and memory with trembling hands. He nearly dropped the phone several times, he was shaking so badly, but he got it back in.

Then he tried it again. "Please, please, please . . ."

The phone flashed blue, and Eric felt his eyes water, he was so relieved. When the home screen loaded, he flipped on the flashlight app and climbed to his feet. He was in a tunnel carved by the furious river. He could barely believe he had survived the fall. He hoped the others were as lucky.

Eric shone the light to either side of him and saw that the narrow bank ran along for another fifty feet or so. He started walking, his shoes heavy with water and his toes numb and stinging. He tried to piece the events together. His mother should have been well down the tunnel by the time the chamber collapsed, but that didn't mean she was safe. Eric thought of her pinned under rocks and felt sick to his stomach.

She's fine, he told himself. *You have to focus.*

How long could he survive on this riverbank? Would they ever find him? He could have been dragged half a mile from where they'd fallen, for all he knew. He thought of Sam Gribley living up on the mountain alone, facing storms and starvation and cold. Sam never let despair take him—to do so would have been certain death. He had to be as strong and stubborn as the mountain itself, and only then did he survive it. Eric would have to do the same down here.

I am not going to die, he thought.

He walked along the shoreline, shining his light on the treacherous footing until he finally came upon a welcome sight: a short, natural opening cut into the stone, dry and still. A tunnel. If he had been stuck beside the river with the constant freezing spray, he would likely have frozen to death. The tunnel gave him a chance.

Eric ducked inside of it, leaving the raging water behind him. Then he stopped, thinking.

Most survivalists said it was smartest to stay where you were. Traveling in unfamiliar terrain was dangerous, and you were supposed to conserve energy. But this was an unusual situation.

Rescuers would have no idea where to find him, and even if the class did survive the river and washed up farther down in the caves, they would never come looking for *him*. He was on his own, and he didn't feel like sitting here in the dark until his phone battery ran out and he froze to death.

No. He was going to find his own way out.

Five Minutes After

THE MAD DESCENT OF THE RIVER SEEMED ENDLESS, and Silvia wondered numbly if she was going to die. She had stopped struggling after the first few minutes, feeling her limbs tiring and her breath growing short and halting in the bitingly cold water. She had quickly learned to float on her back as close to the surface as possible with her legs pointed downstream. Before that, her legs had been battered by the rocks beneath the surface and she had smacked her shoulder off something as well. There was a break in the violent current, and she heard frantic screams and shouts and pleas for help all around her. She wasn't alone, and that gave her hope.

Finally, when the cold had begun to numb her body so much that even the small effort required to float on her back seemed impossible, the deafening roar of the white water began to fade away behind her. She felt herself drift out into motionless water, and she finally allowed her feet to sink down below the surface again so she could tread water.

"Ashley!" Silvia called, her teeth chattering so much she worried they might chip. Now that the current had stopped, the cold seemed even worse; a mixture of burning, tingling, and most dangerously of all, a deep and aching numbness. "Where are you?"

"Here," Ashley called back. Her panicked voice sounded only about twenty feet away. "I'm here! What happened? Where are we?"

Silvia looked around, trying to find the source of Ashley's voice, but it was so dark that she couldn't even tell the water from the air.

"I don't know," she said. "Anyone else?"

A chorus of voices greeted her, shrill or sobbing or quivering from the cold.

"We need to get to shore," Silvia said, treading harder to keep her head out of the water.

If she slipped under, no one would ever find her.

"Spread out!" she heard Jordan call. "Shout if you find something!"

Silvia began to swim, reaching out with every slow, measured stroke. The blindness amplified her other senses, so that she could hear the others' splashing and shallow breathing and feel the cold on every inch of her body like a million stabbing pins. She just had to hope that her eyes would adjust—maybe enough to at least pick out shades and silhouettes. The water smelled clean, though faintly metallic, and with the amount she had swallowed in the tumble down the river, she knew it was fresh water.

Silvia picked up her pace, swimming frog style. Just as her mind was starting to slow from the cold and the despair was starting to creep through her, her right leg kicked ground. Hard, rocky ground. She put her feet down and grinned . . . she could stand. Silvia took a few more steps and realized the bottom was heading steadily upward. Soon the freezing water was falling away from her knees, and then she stepped out completely.

"Hey!" she shouted. "I found the shore. Over here! Follow my voice!"

The sounds of frantic splashing followed, and soon the first of the students started to make their way up the shore. Silvia couldn't see them, but she could hear them as they sloshed onto land. Derek was first, sniffling and hoarse. Then Mary and Marta, still at each other's side. Then Jordan, Brian, Naj, and Joanne. More students emerged from the lake, and they huddled together on the shoreline, sopping wet and freezing. When Ashley came out Silvia wrapped her in a fierce hug, and Ashley sobbed freely into her shoulder.

"I thought I was going to die," Ashley murmured. "I thought I was dead."

"We're out now. It's okay," Silvia said, trying to hold back her own tears.

"What are we going to do, Sil?" she asked. "It's so dark. And I'm so cold."

Silvia paused. "I don't know yet."

"Help me!" someone cried out from the water. It sounded like Shannon. "He's unconscious!"

"Who has a flashlight?" Silvia asked, looking around. "See if it works!"

Everyone started to rummage in their bags or adjust their

flashlight batteries, frantically trying to get them to work. Silvia looked to where she thought the lake was and tried to spot Shannon in the heavy darkness, but it was useless. She couldn't see an inch in front of her.

"Shannon?" she called. "Where are you?"

"Greg's not breathing!" she said. "Help me!"

Behind her, there were relieved gasps as a flashlight suddenly burst into life. It cut through the darkness like a laser beam, shooting upward some thirty yards but fading before it found a ceiling. The huge cavern must have dwarfed the Big Room a thousand times over.

"It works!" Jordan exclaimed.

"Find her!" Joanne said.

He pointed the light out over the lake, and they soon saw Shannon swimming toward the shore, struggling as she pulled an unconscious Greg along behind her with one arm. Joanne hurried out into the water and helped pull him in, while Shannon collapsed on the ground.

"I ran into him on the way," Shannon managed, struggling to catch her breath.

Joanne leaned over Greg, feeling his chest. "He's not breathing!" she said shrilly.

"Greg!" Jordan shouted, blanching. "Someone help him!"

"Does anyone know CPR?" Tom asked.

Everyone looked around for a moment. Silvia was stricken by fear and cold and panic, and hoping desperately that someone, *anyone* else could help. They all stayed quiet.

"Get out of the way!" Silvia said.

She had to try. She had taken a CPR course with her mom last year—her mom thought it might make Silvia feel better about her own issues. She knelt beside Greg, reaching to check for his pulse and then remembering that her instructor said not to waste any time on that step—it was difficult to feel a pulse sometimes, especially right out of the water. Instead, she opened Greg's mouth, stuck her ear against it, and listened for breathing. There was nothing.

"Keep the light on me, Jordan," she said, trying to keep her voice steady.

She started pushing on his chest with two carefully folded hands, counting out loud in rhythm. "One, two, three, four . . ." She made hard, firm compressions, using her full body weight.

When she had done thirty, Silvia put her mouth on his and breathed out before pushing on his chest again. "One, two, three, four, five . . ." Greg lay there lifelessly as she kept pushing.

Silvia kept going, breathing into his mouth again, and with a last violent shove on his chest Greg coughed, spitting out water. As he gasped for air, Silvia sat back, exhausted. She wiped her face with a sleeve as Greg coughed again and tried to sit up. Jordan rushed over to help him, crying out in relief and supporting his shoulders.

"Whoa," Tom murmured, looking at Silvia. "That was amazing."

Silvia felt her cheeks flush. "It was lucky," she said.

"No, it wasn't," Joanne said. "You just saved his life."

Silvia forced a smile and stood up, feeling a little shaky herself. "I guess."

Greg was now sitting up fully while Jordan patted his back,

trying to calm him as he tried to get his rapid breathing under control. Silvia took another count of the group in the glare of Jordan's flashlight. Thirteen people, including her. The only ones missing were Eric, Mr. Baker, and Eric's mom, though Silvia hoped Ms. Johnson had made it far enough down the tunnel to avoid the fall. Mr. Baker and Eric had not been so lucky.

"Everyone try your flashlights again," Silvia said. "We need more light."

She must have dropped hers into the river during the fall.

One by one, flashlights started to flick on. The lights searched across the lake, but found no other walls.

But they weren't trapped. Beyond the narrow, rocky strip of shore where they were standing were four openings cut into the chamber wall. The tunnels were craggy and uneven, but they were all tall enough to walk in upright. They could leave . . . but where would they go?

Silvia looked at the class, bedraggled and soaked. Half of them were in tears, and a few were nursing cuts and bruises. Brian's cut looked dangerously deep. No one besides Mr. Baker had brought Band-Aids or any first aid supplies, so Brian was pressing his T-shirt against his forehead to staunch the blood.

For a while everyone spoke in quiet whispers, letting the tears dry up as they shivered and hugged themselves. Silvia stared out at the water, looking for any hints of movement on the surface. Finally, Tom stepped in front of the group, holding a flashlight under his face.

It made him look grim and ghost-like.

"We need a plan," he said.

"What plan?" Jordan asked. "We're going to sit here until we're rescued, right?"

"We could," Tom said, looking around the massive chamber. "But how long do you feel like waiting for someone to come and save you? Me, I would rather walk the caves. There are tunnels right over there. One of them has to lead upward, or maybe to somewhere warmer. We should at least try."

"We could get lost," Jordan said, sounding unconvinced.

"We *are* lost," Tom replied. "Too late for that. Look around. You want to stay here?"

The flashlights flickered around the cave, falling on still black water and barren stone.

There was a moment of silence, and then Silvia spoke up. "We're forgetting about Eric."

"What about him?" Tom asked, hesitating. "If he didn't make it out of the lake . . . there's not much we can do. We were calling for people . . . he didn't answer. It was a rough trip down, Sil. . . ."

Silvia shook her head. "Eric made it out. I heard him shouting and tried to get to him, but the current was too strong. I think he was on the shore."

"It's true," Brian said, the shirt still pressed to his forehead. "He was trying to reach me."

"Me too," Joanne added. "But I couldn't get to him. He was on dry land."

Tom frowned, shining his light back out over the lake. "He could be way back there."

"I'm sure he is," Silvia said, following his gaze. "And we need to go find him. He could be hurt, and he might not have a flashlight. He was trying to help. We can't just abandon him."

Jordan seemed unconvinced. "How are we going to do that?"

"We'll start by looking," Silvia said dryly. "We'll just head down one of these tunnels. Our voices should carry a long way down here. Besides, we should keep moving. It will warm us up."

A murmur of assent ran through the class.

Tom nodded. "Fine. But we should probably see what supplies we have before we set out. My cell is broken. Won't even turn on or anything. Anyone's working? Any reception?"

The students all took out their cell phones and started to fiddle with the batteries. Only five cell phones turned on, and none of them had any reception. Brian turned his over curiously.

"We are over a thousand feet down," he said. "There is no chance these will work. Even if I could somehow boost them, it wouldn't do a thing. We'd need at least a faint signal. We can keep an eye on them, but it's highly unlikely."

Tom sighed. "What else? Food? Water?"

"What does that matter?" Derek asked. "Everyone gets their own."

"Just call it out," Tom said sharply.

They did a count. Nine flashlights, six granola bars, eight juice boxes, ten water bottles, two Gatorades, four bananas, two chocolate bars, and a peanut butter and jelly sandwich. That was not good. If they were down here for more than a day or two, hunger would soon set in, and some people had brought *nothing* to eat. Silvia wondered who would share if it came to that.

"Is there any food down here, you think?" Mary asked nervously.

Silvia thought about that. "I didn't see anything in the explored areas. And caves in general? There are some mushrooms that are edible, but even if we find some, it would be too risky. There might be subterranean crabs or fish in the water, but how are we going to catch them? How would we cook them if we did? I wouldn't count on finding anything down here."

"I *had* a sandwich," Derek griped, throwing the soggy mess into the lake.

"Are you nuts?" Jordan asked, gesturing at the water. "We need all the food we have."

"Why?" Mary asked fearfully. "Do you think we're going to starve?"

"How long will we be down here?" Shannon said.

"Help!" Brian shouted up at the blackness overhead, the cell phone forgotten.

"Relax," Tom said, holding up his hands. "I'm sure it won't matter. We'll be out of here in no time. A few hours at the absolute most. But just in case, try and go easy on the supplies. Derek, maybe don't waste anything."

"How do you know it will only take a few hours?" Ashley asked.

Tom paused. "I don't. But I'm sure it's fine. They'll get to us, *if* we don't get out of here first."

"So what now?" Derek asked, looking around warily.

Silvia turned to the four tunnel openings. "We choose one of these, and then we walk."

Jordan pulled something out of his backpack.

"Not quite," he said, carefully unfolding a sopping wet map. "I grabbed this a while ago."

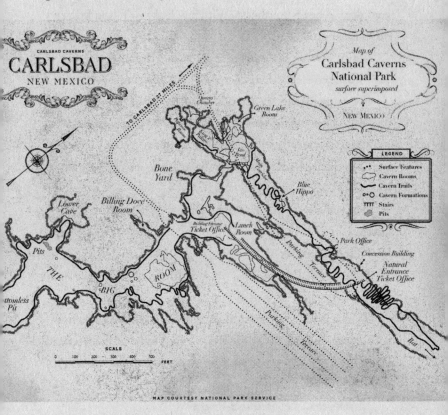

Silvia nodded. "Perfect. So where is the Mystery Room?"

"It's not on here, but it's right off the Queen's Chamber," Jordan said, pointing it out on the map. "If we're going to walk—and for the record, I still don't think we should—we should try and get back toward the middle of the caverns to see if the elevators are still working. They're there beside the ticket office," he continued, tracing his finger to the label. "We also want to go up wherever possible. So we pick the tunnel that goes up and heads southeast. With any luck, we'll find Eric and Mr. Baker on the way."

"Great," Derek said sarcastically. "We'll just follow the sun."

Jordan scowled at him. "Does anyone have a compass?"

Everyone looked at each other blankly.

"Who keeps a compass with them?" Derek asked. "We have GPS."

"Well, the map is still better than nothing," Silvia said, coming to Jordan's defense. "We'll just have to try and figure it out as we go."

"Hey guys . . . ," Brian said, his eyes wide beneath the bloodied shirt.

"What?" Tom asked.

Brian pointed a trembling finger at the water. "The sandwich is gone."

They all shined their flashlights on the lake. Brian was right. There wasn't a trace of the sandwich. Silvia felt a little shiver run down her back. They had all been swimming in there moments before.

"It just sank," Leonard said absently.

"A sandwich?" Jordan replied. "It would have floated."

"It doesn't matter," Tom said, waving his hand in dismissal. "We're out of the water."

He walked toward the tunnel entrances, scanning the four options. Silvia kept her eyes on the water. Jordan was right. It was unlikely that sandwich would have sunk so quickly.

"Which way?" Tom asked aloud, his eyes on the tunnels.

Nobody answered, and instead, one by one, they turned to Silvia. She fidgeted.

"I don't want to choose . . . ," she said uncomfortably.

"Someone has to," Ashley replied. "You pick."

"I'm following you, that's for sure," Greg said weakly, staying close to Jordan.

Silvia awkwardly scratched the nape of her neck. She hadn't expected them to turn to her.

"Well . . . ," she said, walking over to the tunnels and inspecting each one. "This one seems to slope upward, and it's wider too. I don't know if it's southeast, but let's find out, I guess."

The group gathered behind her, and she tentatively accepted Joanne's flashlight.

"I guess I'll go first," Silvia murmured, though they seemed to have already decided that.

As the group filed through the opening, she shone the flashlight up into the tunnel, and the beam stretched far ahead until the passage curved out of sight. There Silvia saw a flicker of movement . . . there and gone before she even blinked. She slowed down, her heart racing. It must have been a shadow. A trick of the light.

But for just a second, she thought she had spotted eyes reflecting the light. Human eyes.

One Hour After

THE TOWN WAS BROKEN. ROCKS HAD FALLEN RIGHT through squat, century-old homes, shattering the fleshy mushroom caps that served as roofs. Other boulders from the distant ceiling had cracked on impact and lay strewn about the street like haga beetle droppings.

Many of the townspeople were injured. A few were dead—already covered with starchy yellow yew leaves and hides until a proper burial ceremony could be arranged. Each would be laid on a raft in the river and carried by the Mother deep into the Earth.

The King watched solemnly from the town square as his people tended to the wounded or cleared the debris, all of them caked with heavy dust. It made them look like stones themselves, or ancient statues come to life. One real statue stood in the middle of the square, watching the scene with cold, disapproving eyes: Juarez Santi, the first Midnight King.

It had been painstakingly carved from limestone and stood ten feet tall.

Medianoche was a small place, and the King knew every villager by name. The town was comprised of one main street with two smaller roads cutting across it, all three lined with one-story structures built of sturdy barbar branches and yew leaves. It was perched right in the center of a great chamber beside a swift, icy river that flowed from the east wall and wound through the cavern like a ribbon. The river gave life to the vegetation on the banks—tall yellow reeds and dense shrubbery that sprouted berries and harbored water lizards, white salamanders, and voles. The town was usually dark, though some burned torches while working or when gathering in the market to feast.

And it always was quiet. Voices were small and shy within the great chasm of darkness, and no one wished to disturb the Mother with undue noise. But it was not quiet today.

The boy King had never seen anything like this before. In the entire recorded history of the Midnight Realm—one hundred and eighteen years—there had never been such a violent shaking. The worst event had been a small flood of Medianoche some eighty years ago when the river burst its banks, and only a few homes had been ruined. None had ever died from such a thing . . . the Mother had never killed anyone directly. Most believed that she would *never* kill one of her children without just cause. And now the King had forced her to punish them.

"Carlos," a soft voice said. He turned, and his little sister rushed into his arms.

Eva was the only one who would dare to call him by his name. She was nine and small for her age, though she was as tough and stubborn as barbar roots, and a gifted archer. He scooped her up and hugged her tightly, inspecting her face for cuts.

"Are you all right?" he asked, hugging her again and only reluctantly putting her down.

She nodded. "The Hall wasn't hit. I was helping Grandmother with the baskets."

Captain Salez stood close by, his sword strapped to his waist—fashioned from bone and honed to a fine edge by endless hours with the whetstone. The captain had a deep gash on his forehead, cutting right across to his eye, but he barely seemed to notice. The captain had been Carlos's father's personal guard as well, and he was resilient and hard as stone.

Eva looked Carlos over, inspecting the deep cut on his arm.

"What was that?" she asked softly.

"I don't know," Carlos said. "The Mother came alive."

He didn't want to tell her about the boy. Not yet.

His men were angry enough. He had caught just a few dark looks from them—fleeting, of course. None would ever dare to challenge him directly. But he knew that many thought their King had brought this calamity on them. Spare a Worm, and the Mother will respond. But could it really be true? Would the Mother be so vengeful?

"We should help," Eva said, looking around the village. "*You* should help."

Carlos nodded. His little sister was wise beyond her years, and as usual, she was right.

"Meet me back in the Hall. Go check on Grandmother."

He started down the main road to find the best place to help, Captain Salez close behind him. The villagers all stopped to bow as he passed, dropping anything they were carrying even as they stood in the wreckage of their homes.

As he walked, his heart grew heavier. There were many gardens in Medianoche: gnarled barbar trees with their thin leaves, yew shrubs, stout mogo plants, and smaller, multicolored mushrooms. Many of them had been destroyed in the rockfall as well, the plants broken and smashed. These gardens served as each family's main sustenance, providing food, clothing materials, and medicine. Losing them would be devastating.

Carlos stopped at a damaged house and began to remove the pile of broken barbar branches and snapped vines, tossing them into the street. Villagers rushed to help him, begging him to rest in the Great Hall, but he waved them all away. Eva was right. His place was here, helping. His father would have been here.

A King is only as good as his weakest subject, his father had said. *Make them all strong.*

As Carlos worked, pulling the destroyed roof away one fleshy, shattered piece of mushroom at a time, he heard an agonized moan from beneath the ruins. There was still someone trapped inside.

"Captain," he said sharply, "help me!"

Together they pulled a man from the house. Carlos pressed

his hands to the man's forehead, staunching the blood. He recognized him as the tanner, Morcho, a slender, quiet man with a thinning patch of gray hair. Luckily, he lived alone.

"Bring me yew leaves!" Carlos shouted, his hands already covered in blood.

As he looked down at the injured man, he wondered again if his soldiers were right. Was this his fault? Had he brought this disaster down on his people?

You are an extension of the Earth, Carlos's father had told him sternly. *Respect the Law, care for the Mother, and protect her people, and the Mother will provide life.*

Carlos had broken the Law, and so broken that chain. Despite his father's warnings, he had shown mercy. But should he regret sparing the Worm? He didn't know, and it made him feel weaker still.

Men and women rushed over with the broad, yellow leaves, which were used for bandaging and clothes. They were starchy and thick, and they soaked up blood quickly and hardened to a mottled brown. Soon Morcho's head was fully wrapped, and Carlos stepped back, his hands shaking. He wiped them on his brown hide shirt, and they left long, crimson stains.

And so the blood is on me.

"You are good to us, Midnight King," one woman, Ula, said. "You must go rest."

"Please rest, Midnight King," another, Hami, agreed.

Carlos stared at his blood-stained hands. "Yes," he said. "I will—"

"My King!"

Everyone turned at the panicked shout. A soldier came rushing through Medianoche, soaked in sweat and breathing hard. It was Santiago, a border guard. "What is it?" Carlos asked.

He stopped, clutching his sides. "I . . . I have seen them."

"Seen who? The Worms?"

"No. They must have fallen in the shaking," Santiago said. "Over ten, I am sure."

"Who?" Carlos demanded.

He met the King's eyes. "New people in strange clothes. They must be from the surface."

Gasps went up behind him. Even the King stiffened.

"Are you sure?" he asked sharply.

"Yes," Santiago said. "They had strange white weapons, brighter than any flame. They burned my eyes, and I was lucky to get away."

Carlos looked beyond the terrified soldier, his mind whirling. Everyone knew that there were people on the surface—the white men that the first King had escaped from. But in the century since, those tales of surface humans had faded into whispered stories and half-believed legends. And now the legends had come alive.

"Gather your men," he said to Captain Salez. "Bring everyone to the Hall."

"They were young," Santiago said, his voice barely above a whisper. "Only children."

The town had assembled in the Great Hall—a room built by the very first Midnight King and his people. A monstrous white mushroom stalk stood in each corner like four pillars of bone, lashed together with vines to create walls that matched the bristly crown worn by every Midnight King. A raised throne had been carved from the rock to overlook the room. There was no ceiling. By tradition the Great Hall always stood open to the darkness, broken only by the blazing fire that stood in the center of the room for light. It had burned there constantly since the days of the first King—representing the never-dwindling power of the Law.

It burned still, untouched by the shaking, but it seemed low and dim to Carlos.

The townspeople began to talk among themselves. It was unusual to speak in front of the King without his consent, but Carlos couldn't blame them. This was a nightmare come to life. He could still remember his father's stories, passed down from one King to the next since the days of Juarez—four generations of unquestioned rulers. It was said the white men burned and dug and pillaged the surface until nothing was left but smoke and ash and bones. None could escape them. They were like haga beetles . . . voracious and deadly.

We must always be on guard for them, his father had warned, lit then by the flickering fire, as Carlos was now. A long scar ran from his right temple to his lip—white and puckered as if it had been drawn on with ground yew paste. His hair was always short and coarse, like black fur, and sometimes it crept down his neck. "One day they may arrive to bring death."

They had finally come, as his father had warned. And Carlos was alone.

Help me, Father. Show me the way to protect our people.

"Did you see anything else?" Carlos asked. "Does anyone else know of them?"

Santiago shook his head. "No . . . it was only me."

"Good," Carlos said. "No Worms?"

"None that I could see," Santiago replied. "The demons were on the eastern shore of the lake."

Captain Salez stepped forward. "With your permission, my King, I will take a small group of soldiers and put them to the spear. We cannot allow these surface creatures to find our village."

Carlos looked at him, and he could see the fear in his captain's usually stoic face. His father had always said that they couldn't allow the surface people to find the Midnight Realm. They would consume it as they did everything else, and the Mother and her people would die.

But these were children. . . .

He turned back to Santiago. "They have not seen our people yet," he said. "Correct?"

"No," Santiago murmured.

"Good," Carlos said, rising to his feet. A hundred people bowed immediately. "They may stay well clear of Medianoche. But they must also be watched, so that they do not disturb the Mother nor come in contact with the Worms. These are my lands. I will go watch them myself."

"My King, it is not safe—" Captain Salez said immediately.

"I will be fine," Carlos replied firmly. "They will not see me. And the fewer of us who go, the better—I can move in shadow. It is good that I should see this ancient enemy for myself. Pull the sentries from our borders. I don't want anyone at risk. Bring them all back to the village."

Captain Salez frowned. "But . . . our borders will be exposed. The Worms . . ."

"Will know nothing of the surface humans," Carlos said. "I am sure they have their own troubles from the quake to deal with. I want no one outside of this city but me and the intruders."

He knew he was pushing the limits of his authority. Some soldiers looked incredulous.

"And if they get past you?" Captain Salez asked.

"Then something has gone wrong," Carlos said, "and I will have failed. If they get to Medianoche, do not allow the demons to come anywhere near the village. Kill them on sight."

Two Hours After

ERIC SLOWLY MADE HIS WAY DOWN A PRONOUNCED dip in the tunnel, staying low and using his hands to guide his descent. If he fell and broke something down here, he would be in deep trouble.

He had been walking for a couple of hours now, and nothing had changed. It was all barren limestone, sometimes veined or speckled with crystal or gypsum, and it continually veered left or right or opened into forks. The downward slopes were particularly troubling, since he knew these caves had been formed by water wearing away the limestone for millions of years, and water only went one way . . . *down*. He would need to find another tunnel very soon.

He was almost to the bottom of the slope when his sneaker slipped off a protruding rock. He lost his balance and slammed hard onto his tailbone, sliding down the last ten feet or so. He came to a stop and groaned, rubbing his sore back and shifting his weight onto his side to take the pressure off. It was already throbbing.

"And I always wanted to go spelunking," he muttered.

Eric crawled over to the nearest wall and propped himself up, taking a deep swig of his water bottle. Absently, he checked his cell phone for service. Nothing. Not even a flicker.

Had his mother made it out before the quake hit? What if she was hurt? What if she was dying? The thought made Eric's stomach turn. It was even worse given the way they'd parted. What if he never saw his mother again and the last thing he ever did was ignore her? He wouldn't be able to live with himself.

They'd had to stick together the last few years, ever since his dad had left. She was his best and only friend sometimes . . . his whole life, really. She worked a lot, but she had always been there to take care of him, even when she had to skip dating or nights with friends. That thought lingered for a minute, and Eric stared up at the stalactites, thinking. It had been years since his dad left, and she was just now thinking about going on her first date. It didn't seem fair. Maybe she was better off without him. Eric felt bile creep up the back of his throat, and he shook his head. No. Now wasn't the time to think about that.

Eric checked his phone again, scowling when he saw there were no bars.

He was at eighty-five percent battery life. The flashlight app was hard on the battery, but he had no choice. Without the light, he would be fumbling blindly and might tumble into a chasm. As for food, he had a raisin granola bar, a can of a tuna, and a water bottle. He had a strange fondness for tuna and usually just ate it plain right out of the can with a fork. It wasn't much food, though . . . a definite concern.

If he was down here for more than a day or two, he would need to find food. Water was seemingly plentiful, though he was worried about bacteria and would have preferred to boil it, if he had a choice. But it was nutrients that he really needed, and cave animals had evolved for thousands of years to find solutions to that problem. He had a few days to figure it out, at most.

Eric climbed to his feet again and kept walking. His clothes were still soaked, and he was freezing. It was better to keep moving. He was hoping to find a volcanic vent with a little heat so he could dry his clothes. He pictured himself slipping into a luxurious, steaming hot spring.

Keep dreaming, he thought, stepping around another protruding stalagmite.

As he walked, he thought about his father. His dad had been a hunter and outdoorsman, and as much as Eric didn't want to admit it, that had led to his appetite for survival stories. He had always wanted to impress his dad when he was younger, and since he didn't play sports, it seemed like the best way. But all the reading and research had kind of backfired on him.

He remembered one night when he was seven. It was winter— he could still remember the frost on the windows. His dad rarely came home right after work, and it used to cause a lot of fights between him and Eric's mom. Eric tried to ignore them, mostly, but that night he hadn't been able to sleep, and so he had cracked his door open and huddled against the frame, listening.

"Where were you?" his mother yelled. It was well past midnight. She always fell asleep on the couch until his dad got home. Even at that age, Eric knew it wasn't normal. The parents on TV slept in the same bedroom. And they didn't scream at each other all the time either.

"Out with the guys," his dad said gruffly.

"You're always out with the guys. Your son asks about you, you know."

"I doubt it. Kid's too busy with his books. You're babying that kid. Messing him up."

Eric had stiffened. They didn't usually talk about him.

Her voice lowered just a little. "There is nothing wrong with him. He is extremely smart."

"Whatever you need to tell yourself. The kid's a loner. No sports. No friends. Nothing."

"He just likes to be alone!" she said.

His dad laughed. "No one likes to be alone. He's weird, Sandra. You know it."

Eric slipped back from the door into the shadows. *Weird.* That's what the kids at school called him too. His mom said they were jealous. But what about his dad?

"Keep your voice down," she said sharply.

"I will. I'm going to bed."

Eric heard his mom try to grab him. "You can't just brush me off."

"Watch me."

As his dad marched upstairs, Eric snuck back to his bed and stared at the ceiling in the dark. It was the first time he believed it, that he was different and odd and maybe even a freak like Derek said last month when Eric was sitting alone in the schoolyard reading *Robinson Crusoe*.

It was a belief that never really went away.

Eric looked up and saw that the tunnel opened about twenty yards ahead, right at the edge of his light. The rock here was a rich brown, colored with layers of black shale and translucent white veins that sparkled like spiderwebs in the morning. He noticed there was also a sheen of dampness in some areas and touched it. Cold, clear water was seeping down the walls. Eric sincerely hoped he wasn't walking under a subterranean river like the one he had just escaped. He stepped around a crack in the ground and emerged from the tunnel into a chamber.

"What . . . ?" he murmured.

There were stars above him. They shone like candles, white and tinged with blue, and they covered the ceiling in a rich tapestry. It was as if he was standing in a quiet country field.

He shined his cellphone light up and something else caught his eye, shimmering in the glare.

There were strands of silk, long and clear and dangling down toward him like fishing lines. There were hundreds of them, though the chamber was so tall that they were still ten yards above him. He realized what he was seeing. *Glowworms*. They had learned about them a few weeks ago. The strange, fleshy creatures sat up on the ceiling, suspended in little hammocks of their own viscous saliva, which they also used to create the long strands. Bugs would fly into them, get caught, and then be slowly consumed by the translucent worms. They even created the lights to attract their prey.

Eric walked beneath them, shining his light over the strands of dangling, deadly saliva.

He was relieved. It meant there was life down here—though he hoped he would never have to eat bugs. He crossed the chamber until he found another small opening in the limestone. He was about to leave again when he had a thought: He might be the first person to ever be here in all the history of mankind. If he made it out again, explorers would want to follow him.

Eric snapped a picture of the chamber with his phone, and then swung his backpack off.

He had a notepad in there and some pens, and he sat down, put his cell phone on the paper for light, and began to draw a map. For one, it meant he was charting the caves and might get to name them—that's how it used to work in the old days, anyway. But more importantly, if he mapped out the caves as he went, he might be able to stop himself from walking in circles.

Eric began to draw. He started with the explored portions and then added to it. The map wasn't pretty, but it showed the general idea.

Of course, the central problem with his map was that he didn't know any directions. His map could be completely backward. If he had a compass, he could make something a little more accurate, but

unfortunately, he didn't. *Something to think about for later*, he decided.

Eric stared at the question mark on his map for a bit, thinking about the class. Were they okay? Were they still being dragged along in that river somewhere, or had they managed to climb out? He didn't want to think about the possibility of a waterfall plummeting down into the blackness. Mr. Baker had said there were underground waterfalls in some cave systems.

But if they were fine, they would be trying to get back to the explored sections . . . it was the only reasonable path. He wondered if they had even noticed he wasn't there. Probably not.

Eric packed up his notebook and stood up again, smiling at the mock stars twinkling electric blue overhead. Despite everything, the chamber was beautiful.

Eric turned and started up the new tunnel, which, thankfully, seemed to slope upward. He kept note in his head of the number of steps and therefore the relative distance. If he was going to start mapping the caves, he might as well be as accurate as possible. As he walked, he examined the type of rock on the walls, always keeping an eye out for white spots. White meant chalk, chalk meant flint, and flint meant at least the possibility of a fire, if he could ever find something to burn. He had just stopped to inspect one misshapen boulder when he heard something.

Eric froze. It was soft and almost imperceptible, but in the heavy silence of the caves, he could still make out exactly what it was—the slow, methodical padding of footsteps in the dark.

Two and a Half Hours Later

SILVIA WAS STARTING TO WONDER IF THEY HAD made the right decision. They had been walking for hours, and the bottoms of her feet were growing sore from the constant pounding on rock. The tunnel had continued to run slightly to the right and upward, as they had hoped, so they had skipped any other openings on the way and kept moving. But Silvia knew the unpleasant truth: It was all guesswork. No one had any idea where they were going.

Silvia glanced back to see how everyone else was faring. Ashley was right behind her, shuffling along with her eyes on the ground, and following her were the twins, Mary and Marta, walking shoulder-to-shoulder in their matching red ball caps that were pulled almost to their eyebrows. They occasionally exchanged whispers, but Silvia could never quite catch what they said. It was probably for the best.

Derek, Leonard, and Tom were behind them, and all three

were debating the exact depth of their location based on the time of the fall and their relative speed in the river. Even Silvia had to admit that their conversations were amusing.

"Bro, you're not accounting for the actual velocity," Leonard said, shaking his head.

"Uh, actually I did," Derek replied smugly. "Did you even listen to my equation, dude?"

"Yeah, and it's wrong. That current was moving *easily* ten miles an hour. Now add that to our initial fall of five seconds—"

"Five seconds?" Derek said incredulously. "That's like falling the length of the entire rink, man. That's crazy."

Leonard threw his hands up in the air, exasperated. "That's what we did. Did you even feel that impact? What do you know about the length of the rink anyway, you're the goalie!"

Derek sounded hurt. "Hey, man, I still skate around the rink during warm-ups! Why do you got to bring that into this? You know I don't like you demeaning my position, bro."

"Yeah, not cool, Leonard," Tom agreed. "And it was a two-second fall."

Silvia bit back a laugh.

Jordan and Greg were next, and Jordan spent most of the walk loudly complaining that they should have stayed by the lake. The quieter students were in the rear—Joanne, Naj, Brian, and Shannon. Once in a while one of them would manage a joke or a sarcastic comment and get a half-hearted laugh from the others, but mostly they walked in grim silence. It felt like a funeral procession.

Silvia shivered at the thought.

"I wish we went to Albuquerque," Ashley said for the tenth time.

Silvia glanced at her. "I wish I was at home on the couch with my cat. Eating ice cream."

"Yeah," Ashley agreed. "Jackson is probably waiting by the door for me for a belly rub."

"Well, we'd better get back soon then," Silvia said, and Ashley managed a wan smile.

It was better than nothing.

"Think we'll actually get out of here?" Ashley asked quietly.

"Of course we will," Silvia said. "And we'll find Eric and Mr. Baker on the way, too."

"Maybe," she replied, sounding dubious. "At least we have you, GI Jane."

Silvia frowned at her. "What are you talking about?"

"You saved Greg's life, Sil."

"I took a course. It was nothing."

Ashley shook her head. "It wasn't nothing. Why don't you go ask Greg? It was, like, the bravest thing I have ever seen. I just didn't know you were like that."

Silvia flushed. "I'm not brave, trust me."

"That's not what—"

"Just leave it, okay?"

Ashley looked a little hurt. "Yeah . . . fine."

Silvia kept walking. She wondered if Ashley would still say that if she saw Silvia when she was alone in the bathroom, crying and struggling to catch her breath.

Silvia wasn't brave. She had just gotten lucky, and now she was stuck as the leader.

She noticed that the tunnel walls seemed damp now, as if covered in a shimmering morning dew. That was odd enough, but she soon noticed something far more unexpected: Sporadic patches of moss and lichen were popping up, clearly feeding off the dampness.

"That's weird," she said. She stopped in front of a particularly thick green patch.

Silvia lightly brushed her hand through some of the moss—it was dense and spongy and damp, and she saw something with a lot of legs scurry away from her fingers. She quickly pulled her hand back, surprised, and then tried to follow the creature with her light. It looked like a centipede, mostly black with a few yellow lines running across its carapace. It was also at least six inches long—bigger than any insect she had ever seen. The creature settled beside another patch, seemingly munching on the moss.

"Great," Ashley muttered, staying well back of it. "Giant bugs."

Silvia leaned close. The centipede had no eyes, and its legs were long and spindly.

"It is good, actually. It means there is life, even this far down. Life means food."

"You want to eat that?" Ashley asked, sounding disgusted.

Silvia laughed. "Well, we'll start with our snacks. And no . . . I don't want to eat a centipede. But he's eating something. This moss must have some nutrients. We'll see."

She kept moving again, and Ashley hurried after her. They

soon emerged into a chamber about the size of their classroom, pockmarked with some rust-colored columns and stalactites.

There were three tunnel openings carved into the wall ahead of them. Silvia stopped.

Jordan stepped up beside Silvia, examining his map. He turned it around a few times, trying to get his bearings, and then seemed to get frustrated. "Well, we don't really know which way the river flowed originally. I still think it was parallel to the opening for the Mystery Room, which means south. If so, we could be somewhere around here," he mused, tracing his finger along the map thoughtfully. "Tough to say. We could even be under the Bone Yard, I guess."

"That's comforting," Mary said.

"So where do we go now, genius?" Tom asked.

Jordan scowled. "Hey, this wasn't my idea. These sections aren't on the map."

"Well, you've done a whole lot of complaining," Tom said. "I figured you might know something."

"Yeah," Jordan said sharply. "When you're lost . . . stay where you are!"

"If you're a wuss," Tom snarled.

Silvia stepped between them, raising her arms. They couldn't afford to lose their cool down here. "Not helping, Tom. Jordan, we *all* decided to leave and look for Eric."

"I didn't," Jordan said, handing Silvia the map. "Here. You have any ideas?"

Silvia stared at it for a moment. If Jordan was right, which was a big *if*, they needed to go north to get back to Eric, and east to head back toward the elevators. Should they put it to a vote?

What does it even matter? she thought. *We need to know the directions.*

"Any ideas on figuring out directions?"

They had already checked for compass apps on their three working cell phones, but nobody had one—they all relied on GPS. Silvia knew that moss always grows on the north side of trees, but the moss down here didn't seem to follow any sort of pattern.

"Can't we build a compass?" Naj asked. "I'm sure there's a way."

"I don't remember how," Leonard said. "You need a cork and a magnet, I think. But I heard once that people always find their way north if they try. Not always, but, like, as a majority."

Jordan frowned. "Where did you hear that?"

"I don't know. I just did. When I say *go*, everyone point where they think is north."

"Are you sure about this?" Silvia asked skeptically.

Leonard ignored her. "No. One, two, three, go!"

Everyone immediately pointed. Silvia couldn't help but laugh. Everyone had pointed in different directions.

Leonard seemed nonplussed. He did a quick count, averaging out the pointing hands into general directions. "Four of us this way—a clear favorite. This is north." He pointed at the rock wall on the right of the chamber, and slumped when he saw there were no openings. "Figures."

"That was the worst experiment I have ever seen," Mary said.

"Hey, it's better than nothing," Leonard replied indignantly, flushing pink.

"Let's try this one," Silvia said, pointing to a wide, squat tunnel with smoother floors than the other two. "If we can turn right at some point, we'll take a look; okay, Leonard?"

He nodded, mollified.

"Let's take a quick water break," she said. "We'll leave in ten minutes."

Everyone gratefully took out their water bottles and idled around the chamber, which Brian named the Rust Room. Silvia took a drink and stared at the openings, trying to decide if her choice was a good one. The smartest choice might well be to split up and send people down all of them, but no one would agree to that. Even she didn't like it, whether it was the smartest choice or not. She took another drink and sighed. And that's when she spotted something on the wall. She leaned closer to have a look.

"Guys . . . come here."

Three Hours After

ERIC SLOWLY STRAIGHTENED UP AND SWEPT HIS
cell phone light in all directions. The footsteps halted, and
silence fell again.

He scanned the tunnel, wishing that he had a real flashlight. The dim light from his cell phone stretched only ten yards
or so and cast everything into an eerie white glow. Eric took
a few tentative steps forward, every muscle in his body alert.
His breathing sounded loud and ragged in his ears, even as he
fought to stay quiet. He heard more footsteps approaching, and
then something else entirely . . . short, rapid *sniffing*. The noise
was behind him.

Eric whirled around. His light fell on two beady black eyes.

They were attached to the biggest rat he had ever seen. It was
the size of a Beagle, covered with coarse, filthy brown fur, and it
had a long prehensile tail that stretched some three feet behind it
like a snake. As it sniffed the ground, its mouth suddenly cocked

open and Eric caught a glimpse of long yellow teeth. That was enough to break his moment of shock.

Eric screamed and jumped back, startling the enormous rat. It took off down the tunnel again, moving unnervingly fast. In a matter of seconds, it had vanished entirely.

Eric stood there for a moment, breathing hard. He had been hoping to find life down here, but he hadn't been expecting *that*. He would have to be very careful when going to sleep. That rat was big enough to take a chunk out of his face.

Taking another quick look around, Eric brought out his notebook and pen. He figured it would be worthwhile to document the animals he found, too. He optimistically drew the tunnel he was in as leading back toward the explored sections.

He closed the notepad and put it away, feeling like a true explorer. He wondered if they would ever use Super Rat as a scientific term. Probably not. Maybe *Rattus superatus*.

Eric reluctantly started down the tunnel after the rat, hoping they wouldn't meet again. He checked his phone battery as he walked and saw that he was down to seventy percent now. That was bad.

Making sure to watch his footing, Eric moved slowly down the tunnel. The ground was uneven and pockmarked with stalagmites and crevices that would surely catch his shoe if he wasn't careful. He continued to examine the rocks as he went, eager to find some flint. It was still mostly limestone here, as with most caves, but there was a lot of shale and even some areas that looked like they could be granite, so clearly the geology of the caves changed as he got deeper.

But how had there been a rat?

That was puzzling him. Animals needed nutrients to survive, but there was no sunlight or food here and no conceivable way to get to it. They had studied a bunch of cave animals that had adapted to find food in other ways. Roaches and crabs and some small mammals survived off bat guano, and bats left the caves to find food. Other animals, like cave snakes, just ate the bats and got their nutrients that way. But what would the rat eat? Were there bats nearby? Maybe he was closer to escape than he thought, and his map was completely wrong. Eric suddenly did a double take, and then came to an abrupt stop, frowning.

He had been searching for spots of white on the walls, and he had finally found one.

But it wasn't what he was expecting. It was a crude, uneven M.

Eric knelt down beside the mark and ran his fingers over it. It was bumpy and dry, like it had been drawn on with some sort of paste. He felt his skin prickle as he snapped a picture of it.

Had someone been down here already? The class? Mr. Baker?

He made a note of it on his map and then stood up, looking warily at the symbol.

It made him uneasy. He decided to get moving again. He picked up his pace, taking another sip of water as he walked. His stomach was growling, but he wasn't ready to start eating his scant supplies yet.

The tunnel began to descend once again and the sides became smoother and garnished with spots of moss. Eric examined the spongy, dense vegetation thoughtfully, wondering if he could eat it. He tore a bit off and put it into his bag . . . he wasn't willing to try it just yet. The fact that it was surviving down here without sunlight was extraordinary, but it might be converting something else into energy—and he wasn't sure it would be healthy.

He did make one welcome discovery: chalk. It appeared on the walls beside him, and as he knelt down to take a closer look, he saw that it was flaking off. *Flint.* He knew it immediately. He used some other loose rocks to knock some free, and then tested it with a fork from his backpack.

Sparks flared in the darkness, and he grinned. He didn't have anything to light, but it was a start. Every survivalist knew that having fire was essential. He tucked the flint into his bag.

As Eric kept moving, the moss grew thicker, until there was a carpet beneath his feet. A few times he thought he saw something move at the edge of his light, but he never got a clear sight. *Maybe the rat was eating moss*, he thought. There was certainly enough of it down here.

The tunnel curved ahead, and Eric kept his light on the ground as he walked, amazed by the thick moss. He turned the corner, his eyes fixed on the ground, and then he felt the air change. It suddenly smelled thick and earthy and fresh, and somehow seemed even more quiet.

Eric looked up. His eyes widened.

"Impossible," he whispered.

Three and a Half Hours After

SILVIA RAN HER FINGERS OVER THE SYMBOL, FEELING her skin crawl. A distinct M had been written on the wall with white paste. It made no sense, and for the first time since the earthquake, she felt the fear taking over. It began to swell, and she felt her stomach turn and her breath shorten and the tingles begin in her fingertips. Silvia looked around, but it seemed that the others gathering around were dismissive.

"Just the way the rock formed," Ashley said. "Cool."

Silvia frowned. It didn't look natural to her. It looked like writing. She felt the texture.

"It's dry and almost flaky," she said. "It doesn't feel like rock to me."

Shannon knelt down beside her. "What do you think it is?"

"I don't know," Silvia said. "But I think it was drawn here."

As she spoke, her eyes scanned every shadow. Suddenly they all seemed alive, writhing and grasping at the edges of her flashlight. Was there something living in the darkness?

Tom frowned. "By who?"

"I don't know," she said, "but I doubt it was Mr. Baker or Eric."

Silvia's whole body was shaking. She tried to calm herself. *Focus on the fear. Allow it. Remember to breathe. Slowly now. The fear is a natural thing. You have dealt with it before.*

Relax.

Tom gave her a patronizing smile. "It's not a drawing, Sil. You're just scared and—"

"Yes, I am," Silvia said sharply. "But it's still a drawing. Thanks anyway."

It came out harsher than she'd intended, and Tom took a step back, hurt visible on his face. Silvia wanted to say sorry, but she was still feeling shaky, so she just turned back to the M. Maybe Tom was right. It was just a natural formation, and she was over-reacting because that's what she did. A sudden memory came back to her from a few years earlier.

"Open wide, Silvia," Dr. Proust said, sticking the dry wooden stick down her throat.

She did as she was told, her mom and dad watching carefully.

"Looks normal," he said, smiling. "We'll do some blood tests. But you're just fine, dear."

Silvia looked at her mom for support. How could she be just fine? She could see her dad smiling and nodding. It was exactly what he wanted to hear. It was nothing. She was normal.

Her mom spoke up. "But, Dr. Proust, she said she was dizzy. She almost threw up."

Dr. Proust returned to his notepad, sitting back in his old chair with the tattered green fabric and cotton seeping through the rips. He had been her doctor since she was a baby. She trusted him. But what he was saying didn't make any sense. How could she be fine after being so sick? How could it just be nothing?

"Maybe just a passing thing. Her vital signs are normal."

Silvia shifted on the table. "But . . . but it happened a bunch of times now."

"We'll do the blood tests," he assured her. "Don't worry. It's just a little phase."

She tried to believe it as they walked out of the office. And when they stuck a needle in her arm for the blood tests. And a week later when they called to say everything was normal.

It was just a little phase, they told her. Two years later, it was still happening.

Tom was standing beside her now, clearly still offended. "Let's just stay calm," he said a bit coolly. "We have enough problems down here without speculating about signs. Okay?"

Silvia nodded, though it was more to apologize to him than anything. "Yeah. Fine."

"So which tunnel?" Jordan asked.

Silvia turned back to the tunnels and paced in front of the openings, still nervous about the symbol. Tom was right though. It wouldn't be a good idea to panic now . . . especially for her.

"Well, natural or not, let's hope it's a sign to go this way," she said.

"You sure?" Derek asked.

Silvia snorted. "No. But unless someone has a better idea, we'll follow the clue."

She started down the passageway, taking a last look at the mysterious M.

Four Hours After

OFFICER DANIEL BROWN LOOKED AROUND THE BUS, thinking of his own daughter. There was something eerie about an empty school bus, he decided. It was supposed to be full of laughter. This one felt like a morgue.

He had called home right after the earthquake to check in, and thankfully, everything was fine there. They had a felt a little tremor in town and nothing more, though his daughter had been sent home from school. She was just happy for the extra day off. It seemed the students of Mr. Baker's class were not so fortunate.

The guides and other employees in the caverns had followed protocol and managed to lead the other visitors out through the natural entrance. But the guides suspected the students were deep inside the caverns when it happened—the last sighting of them had been in the Queen's Chamber, and that area was hit particularly hard.

He glanced out the nearest window to look at the sandstone

visitor center perched in the middle of the desert. A full collapse, the guides had said. Shattered walls and falling stalactites. Even the bats had fled in a great plume, like ash from a volcano. The officer shook his head and walked back to the front of the bus. He was already tired.

He scooped up a sheet of paper from the dash and saw that it was an attendance list.

That's something, at least, he thought. It would make the process easier.

He took a pen out and sat down, scribbling a little note at the bottom. It seemed callous, but it was the prudent thing to do. They had to start contacting families and get them down here. They had to prepare them for the worst.

"Hey, Dan," his partner, Mel, called out, poking her head in the bus. "We got something."

He hurried out of the bus to see a squad car pull up. The back door flew open and a frantic woman emerged, caked in so much dust that he could barely distinguish her features.

"They found her at the natural entrance," Mel said. "She was with the class."

Officer Brown glanced at his partner in surprise and then hurried over.

"Are you okay, ma'am?" he asked, taking her arm.

Tears had turned the dust on her cheeks to clay. She nodded. "Fine. My son . . ."

"Were you with the class?" he asked immediately. "Are you Ms. Johnson?"

"Yes . . . my son, Eric . . ."

Officer Brown quickly turned the attendance sheet away from her so she couldn't read his scribbled note. "When did you last see them, Ms. Johnson?"

"They were in the Mystery Room," she said, wiping her eyes. There was some blood caked on the side of her head. "I heard the quake and tried to get back. It was all collapsing."

She looked at him, her eyes wide.

"I heard them screaming."

Officer Brown grimaced. "As soon as it is stable, we'll send people in."

"When will that be?" she asked, stepping back warily.

"They're watching the seismometer readings now. There could be aftershocks. It's not safe to go in."

"My son is down there!" she snarled. She turned to head for the visitor center.

"The elevators are shut down," Officer Brown said. "And they won't let you back in the other entrance either. We will take care of it, ma'am. Mel, get some paramedics over here—"

The woman turned back to him, and her eyes instantly fell on the attendance sheet.

"The teacher, Mr. Baker, he would be with them," she said. "What does that say?"

Officer Brown tried to put the sheet away. "We'll find them, ma'am. Don't worry."

She snatched the sheet out of his hand. As she read it, her eyes filled with tears.

"No," she murmured. "No, no, no."

"Just a precaution," he said, suddenly feeling very guilty. "Nothing more."

Mel put her arm around Ms. Johnson and took the attendance sheet. Officer Brown gave it to another officer and stepped away, feeling sick. He couldn't imagine what she was going through. He would be inconsolable too and probably half-mad. But he still had a job to do.

The other officer stepped up behind him. "You want me to contact the school? I can tell them to start calling all the parents and get them down here."

Officer Brown nodded. "Yeah. It's time."

Five Hours After

ERIC STEPPED INTO THE CHAMBER, SHINING HIS LIGHT in front of him with disbelieving eyes. The chamber looked enormous—easily a hundred times bigger than the Big Room. And it was *alive*.

His cell phone light didn't reach the ceiling or the walls, but it did fall on the last thing he was expecting to find this far into the Earth: a forest.

It wasn't a forest like any he had ever seen. The trees were squat and gnarled, with thin, needle-like leaves, and they were interspersed with huge mushrooms that stood at least ten feet tall and had enormous caps the size of his bedroom. They were also brilliantly colored: milky white, crimson, garish yellow, emerald green. But most bizarre of all were the shorter, slender mushrooms peppering the space between the giants; they were *glowing* with a dim, electric blue light. There were thousands of them, lighting the forest like candles.

Eric grinned. The mushrooms had evolved bioluminescence, just like the glowworms.

The underground world was not so dark after all.

As he approached the forest, he saw that the vegetation was thick and close. Moss-covered vines hung off the branches like dusty cobwebs, making them seem old and tired and dirty. Smaller mushrooms and yellow bushes with wide, starchy leaves were sprouting up between the trees, creating a dense underbrush. Eric scanned both directions with his cell light, but the forest stretched out like an impassable wall, blocking his way.

He stared at it for a long time, wondering how all this was possible. It explained the enormous rat . . . that was for sure. There could be an entire self-sustaining ecosystem in there.

He noticed something else: the silence. There was no breeze to rustle the leaves, no crunch of fallen leaves, no reassuring birdcalls from the canopy. It was like the ghostly memory of a forest, long dead and now reclaimed by the fungi.

Eric took a picture with his phone and grimaced when he saw he was already down to fifty percent battery. He had a few hours left at most with the light on. He decided to take advantage of the light from the mushrooms and turned the cell phone off.

He took out his notepad and drew the forest onto his map, pausing at the name. He decided on the Mushroom Forest until he could come up with something better. He had no idea how big it was, and left the boundaries unfinished with a question mark.

Eric wondered if this forest would become world famous when he emerged with his photos and his map. He pictured it crawling with scientists and tourists—the noise and lights and crush of civilization. It seemed wrong.

He put his bag down and weighed his options. If he wanted to keep moving, he had to either find his way around the forest, go back, or go through. And he was very curious to go in.

"First, it's time to warm up," he said aloud.

He wandered over to the edge of the woods and ran his hands over the stalk of one of the giant mushrooms: It was moist and fleshy, like his skin after a long bath. The stems were easily three feet around, sometimes more, and they were as stable and rigid as a tree trunk.

He began to gather brush and sticks from the edge of the woods, snapping some off from the gnarled trees, though they were very sturdy and stubborn. After a few trips, he was sweating profusely, but he had managed to gather a pile of tinder and some decent-size limbs for a fire. He built a small teepee from the limbs and stuffed the tinder material inside.

"Here goes nothing," he muttered.

He took the pieces of flint out and began striking one with his fork. He hit it again and again, close to the driest brush he could find, creating a shower of sparks, but it didn't catch. Eric frowned and dug into his backpack. He found an essay that Mr. Baker had returned a few days ago about the role of self-identity in *A Prayer for Owen Meany*. He had gotten an A.

"Oh well," he said, crumpling the paper up. "Sorry, John Irving."

He struck the flint again, and finally, when his fingers were aching, the sparks caught. The paper lit up, and he quickly blew on it and moved the lit paper into the center of the teepee with the dry twigs he had collected. Soon a small fire was blazing, pushing back the shadows and the damp.

Eric slipped off his shoes, setting them open-faced toward the blaze and sticking his socked feet beside them. He rubbed his hands by the flames, feeling the chill fade away.

When he had warmed a bit, he took out one of his granola bars and rewarded himself with half and a few sips of water. He ate the bar slowly, relishing it and leaning back. It felt good to be off his feet.

He almost felt like he was camping. His dad had occasionally taken Eric on hunting trips—even as far as the Pacific Northwest. A love for the outdoors was something they had in common, so Eric always jumped at the chance to go. It was the only time they spent together.

When he was nine his dad took him on a duck hunting trip with his friend Phil, who was a loud, belligerent man with an overgrown beard. At one point, they had gone to follow some tracks and asked Eric to stay behind. His dad said they would move faster without him.

After a while Eric had gotten impatient and went to find them. It wasn't long before he was thoroughly lost. He had panicked and searched until night had fallen black and cool across the forest. Finally, Eric smelled smoke and found his way back. His dad and Phil were casually sitting by the campfire, preparing dinner.

"Not bad," his dad said when Eric emerged from the woods with tears in his eyes. "See, Phil? He can find his way out here. Not an athlete, maybe, but he's got a knack for hunting, I think."

"He didn't even want to touch the duck when you shot it," Phil said, laughing.

His dad snorted. "True. Sit down, Eric. Want to learn how to clean a bird?"

Eric nodded, too afraid to say that he didn't. He watched the grisly process in silence.

"Now we eat," his dad said. "You can try the wing."

He slapped the bloodied wing onto the little spit they'd built and watched it cook. Eric watched the fire, wondering if the dead duck had anyone looking for him. He didn't eat it.

"I thought you wanted to be a hunter, boy?" his father said, looking disappointed.

Eric wanted to eat it. He wanted to make his dad proud. But the blood had turned his stomach, and he just ate some of the wild potatoes they'd found instead. Phil laughed and said Eric clearly wasn't going to be much of a hunter after all, and Eric didn't ever get invited again.

A year later his dad was gone, and there were no more hunting trips anyway.

If only he could see me now, Eric thought. *He'd be proud if he saw me down here.*

The thought made him angry. Why did he care what his dad thought? He had abandoned Eric and his mom and gone off with his new family. He didn't want Eric, and Eric didn't need him either. He didn't need anybody. Eric looked around the chamber and then put his shoes on.

He had made his decision.

He was going through the forest.

Six Hours After

CARLOS MOVED QUICKLY THROUGH THE TUNNELS, HIS rat-hide hunting boots silent upon the rock. He was already midway through the Warrens—a chaotic mass of tunnels that lay between the city of Medianoche and the Ghost Woods. The constant bends and dips and endless openings were difficult to navigate, but Carlos had grown up in these passages.

He carried a jagged knife strapped to his waist—about the length of a forearm and sharpened from black stone. On his back he bore the century-old King's Sword, a three-foot-long blade fashioned from the spine of a monstrous Night Rat—one of the omega predators in the caverns. Not *the* omega predator though, unfortunately.

Carlos had to hope the surface humans stayed well away from the Black Deaths.

As he moved, he thought about his sister. She had begged to come with him.

"I am just as fast as you," Eva said, pouting with her arms crossed. "Probably faster."

Carlos was busy giving his sword a last sharpening in the Great Hall, and he laughed.

"I don't doubt it," he replied. "But it is too dangerous."

She stamped her foot. "It's too dangerous to go alone. You heard the captain."

"He is the captain . . . and I am the King," Carlos said. "It is my decision."

"Well, it's the wrong one."

Carlos admired the blade and slung it over his shoulders, turning to her.

"You just want to see the surface humans," he admonished.

Eva shrugged. "Maybe."

"They are a plague," he said firmly. "You heard Father speak of them. They are deadly."

Eva looked into the fire, frowning. "Will you really kill them if they find Medianoche?"

"If I have to. It is what Father would do—"

"Father is not here," she said quietly, the light playing tricks on her face. "You are."

The words hung in the air for a moment, and Carlos watched a scorched barbar branch crack and split into glowing embers. Then he pulled her into a hug. "I'll see you soon, Eva."

And so he had left alone, feeling many eyes on his back as he disappeared into the tunnels. The truth was he needed to go alone. He needed to feel the Mother's presence again.

He needed to apologize and ask for mercy for his people.

His ancestors had a sacred spot in the Ghost Woods that he was making for now. He would ask for wisdom, and *then* he would find the surface humans. The thought of them made him shiver. The legends described them clearly: white skin turned red by the great burning fire in the sky, tall and broad like giants, weapons called guns that killed instantly, and a ceaseless thirst for death. They killed plants and animals and men like it was nothing. Mothers told children stories of them in their beds, and the children quaked. And now he was going to see them. Alone.

Carlos half-walked, half-slid down a sudden decline, and finally emerged into the cavernous chamber that housed the Ghost Woods. It shone an inviting blue, lit as always by the torch mushrooms. The forest stretched several miles across, and it was the richest source of food and supplies in the entire Midnight Realm.

Carlos had once hated these woods. He had been left here alone for a week when he was just five years old—a grooming process to become the Midnight King. It had been the worst week of his life. Nights alone with silent trees, the calls of hunting lizards, and bugs crawling across his chest and face. By the end, he had felt like an animal too, and his father told him that was the point.

But in time his feeling had changed. He had grown to love the Mother's sanctuary, and he came here still to hunt with his soldiers. The Ghost Woods were the living, breathing spirit of the Realm.

Carlos entered the trees, still barely making a sound in the thick undergrowth. He picked his way around a thicket of stout barbar trees. Vines hung from every limb, ethereal and caked with pollen. They looked like crystalline spiderwebs.

Carlos breathed in the pungent air. He always felt more connected to the Mother here.

As he cut through the undergrowth, he saw other residents of the forest flit from his path. There were many lizards here, most sightless and harmless, as well as long green snakes that hung among the vines for camouflage, bats that filled the canopy, tree mice and voles beneath his feet, and countless numbers of insects—ants, roaches, and large centipedes. The Night Rats hunted here as well, but they would not bother Carlos.

Time passed silently beneath the trees, until Carlos finally stepped out from the underbrush into a clearing. It was a large natural circle in the center of the forest, and in the middle was a crystal clear pool—the final resting spot of the great water that had first carved this chamber. Lilies and water plants floated there, but nothing clouded its pure water.

Carlos laid down his sword and knife and sat cross-legged on the bank. He stared out at the water, dipping his hands in and taking a drink.

"It is I, Carlos Juarez Santi," he said softly, "fourth Midnight King of the Realm."

He looked into the water, seeing only impenetrable blackness.

"I am lost," he whispered. "The Law is paramount. And yet . . . I could not kill that boy. I have failed as a King, and you have punished us."

He paused.

"And now a greater danger has come. Did you bring the surface humans? Do they come to destroy us too? Why did they send children? How can I protect my people?"

He stopped, thinking of his father. He used to take Carlos here, and they would sit for hours by the water, listening to the quiet. Carlos could almost see him, his strong arms draped over his legs. He could sit there without moving, like he had grown into a tree.

"Why must I always fail him?" he whispered—to the Mother, to his father, to no one.

He sat there for some time, his eyes shut. But the silence was not complete today. He heard bats screeching. Animals clawing through the woods. And somewhere . . . clumsy footsteps.

Carlos opened his eyes . . . and saw light.

Six and a Half Hours After

SILVIA STUMBLED OVER A CREVICE, FEELING her ankle roll, and grimaced. Her feet were aching already, and now she had a bum ankle on top of everything else. The tunnel she had chosen had gone up for a bit, then leveled. Now they were heading downward—it seemed like nothing was going right. And she was the leader; she was to blame. The passageway seemed endless, and for all she knew, they were heading toward the molten core of the planet. It even felt warmer, though that might have been psychological.

They had taken a quick break an hour earlier, eating sparingly and drinking more of their precious water. She knew what the class was thinking; she was thinking it too:

Where are we going?

I think this is the wrong way.

My feet are so sore.

I'm freezing. We need a fire.

We're going to run out of food.

They were moving single file through the tunnel now, which was at least smooth and tall enough that they didn't have to crouch. The panic had continued to grow and build in Silvia's stomach, until it seemed like it was pressing on the back of her throat and threatening to erupt.

Even Ashley had fallen silent now, though she stayed close on Silvia's heels. She had broken down crying during the last break, saying they would never get out of the caverns alive.

Silvia had been forced to tell her to keep quiet before she started a general panic.

"You okay?" she asked now, glancing back at her best friend.

Ashley looked pale, and there was sweat beading on her forehead.

Ashley nodded miserably. "Fine. Sorry about before."

"No . . . I should have been more supportive. I just . . . well, I'm scared too. We all are."

Even whispering, their voices carried through the tunnel. She noticed people listening.

"But we'll be fine," Silvia continued. "We're going to start going up again soon."

"We're lost, Sil," Ashley said. "We could be anywhere."

I know, Silvia thought. "As long as we head upward, we'll be fine," she replied instead.

She turned back, shining her light down the tunnel. There was an upward slope now, but it was negligible . . . five degrees at most. At this rate, they could be walking upward for ten years.

She wondered how Eric was doing. Had he escaped the river-bank? Was he alone and scared somewhere? Did he have food or a light or anything at all? She thought about being down here without one and shivered. But the class had walked and shouted his name for almost an hour, their voices echoing down holes and passageways, and they had gotten no response at all.

If he was alive, he was far away.

She noticed that the tunnel was now speckled with white spots. The spots began to jut out in crystalline fragments like icicles, reflecting her flashlight and sparkling brilliantly. She heard a crack and turned to see that Tom had broken off a large piece with the butt of his flashlight.

He saw everyone looking and shrugged. "Just in case it's valuable," he said.

A few more people followed suit, but Silvia decided against it. She was fairly sure it was gypsum.

When the group was done collecting their stones, they moved again. The sparkling stones became more frequent still, and then Silvia's flashlight beam suddenly lit up ahead, as if it had hit a mirror. Frowning, she picked up her pace, and when she emerged into the chamber, she almost laughed.

It was the most beautiful place she had ever seen.

White stone covered the walls and floors and ceilings in magnificent, elaborate formations. It was as if they had wandered into a cathedral of ice, and it all caught the light and sparkled and glowed.

"Wow," Ashley murmured, stepping up beside Silvia.

"Yeah," Silvia agreed.

The class filed out of the tunnel behind her, and she heard one sharp intake of breath after another. Silvia gently ran her hands along one of the white stalagmites, feeling the cool surface. Those who had working phones were taking photos, and the room filled with flashes.

She soon noticed that there were openings cut into the walls—more tunnels to choose from. One led sharply upward. Silvia smiled. Maybe their luck was finally beginning to turn.

"Maybe the caves aren't all bad," Ashley said, staring up at an enormous chandelier-like formation.

"Yeah," Silvia said. "This spot kind of makes up for the rest. The Cave of Diamonds."

Ashley smiled. "I like that. Mr. Baker would have loved to see—"

She was cut off by a scream.

Silvia spun around. Shannon was standing by one of the tunnel openings cut into the walls. She was shaking violently, pointing.

"What happened?" Silvia asked.

Shannon turned to her, her eyes wide. "Brian . . . he's gone."

Seven Hours After

ERIC SLOWLY RAN HIS FINGERS OVER THE SYMBOL, feeling the hairs on the back of his neck standing up. Another M. This one had been carved into one of the white mushroom stalks with a knife.

There was no way this one was natural. Someone had put it here.

Had explorers actually been here before? Had someone else been trapped by the earthquake? Could it have been Jim White or the Kid? But what did the M stand for?

He took a picture of it and drew it on his map in the middle of the unfinished forest.

When he was done, he began moving again, trying to stand as straight as possible. But it wasn't easy. The undergrowth was thick and grasping, and vines, frail as dandelion wisps and covered in pollen, made it hard to see. He had to keep rubbing it out of his eyes with his sleeves.

It was much warmer in the forest, and a little humid as well.

He had tried to figure out how this was all possible, and his best guess was that water from the surface was filtering down into the cavern from a river or stream, packed with bacteria and nutrients, while at the same time some volcanic activity under the forest was heating it all up to create the damp, close air in here.

He snapped more and more pictures as he went, until he saw the battery life: thirty-five percent.

He quickly tucked his phone away again. Once he was out of these glowing woods, he would need the light. But he still wasn't quite as nervous about it as before. The mushrooms provided more than enough light for him to pick his way through the forest, and he could always take some of those with him. He also knew he could make fire now, so a torch was possible too.

As he walked, he saw a speckled gray and black lizard scamper up a tree. There were plenty of those here, most a few inches long. He had also seen green, wiry snakes dangling from the canopy, which had been a little startling at first, but they quickly retracted back into the leaves when they saw him. There were even occasional rodents scurrying through the brush, moving lightning fast.

The forest was teeming with life.

Eric passed a bush covered with small black and red berries. He considered packing some away, but he was leery of any berries he couldn't identify. There were also many fruiting trees that had something that looked like figs hanging from their limbs, and he did put two of those in his bag. Still, he would have to be pretty desperate to try them.

And then he came across something far, far better. As he was walking, his right foot kicked something hard and round that bounced off into the trees. Frowning, he glanced down. Then he quickly took his cell phone out again and flicked on the light for a better view.

"Bingo," he whispered.

The area was littered with wild potatoes. He might have walked right by them, but many had already been dug up by some grazing animal, and a few uneaten potatoes were exposed. Eric scooped them up, stuffing them into his bag, and then pulled out some of the other plants as well. The large potatoes were a mix of gold and deep purple, and he stuffed ten of them into his backpack, wondering if he could create a stone pot to boil them or bake them over some embers.

Eric decided it was a good spot for a break, and he sat down right in the clump of potatoes, taking his shoes off and massaging his feet. He took out his water bottle and had a deep drink, no longer as concerned with water conservation either. He was starting to feel more and more like Sam Gribley on his mountain. If Eric just had a falcon to do his hunting for him, he'd be set. The thought lingered for a moment. Not the falcon . . . but the mountain. That mountain was Sam's personal kingdom . . . just him and the wild. He answered to nobody. He didn't have a schedule. He was completely free.

And here was Eric, deep in the Earth. Not on a mountain, but in a living, breathing hole.

He was independent here. He didn't need anyone. It was exactly what he had always wanted.

He thought back to the day his father left. It was a Saturday morning in October. It was cool for New Mexico, and he had woken cold, wrapping himself in a blanket. His mom was at work, so his dad was watching him, like he always did on Saturdays. But it was still early, and Eric already heard some movement by the door, which was strange. His dad usually liked to sleep in late on the weekends, unless he was going hunting. But he hadn't said anything.

Eric walked downstairs and saw two suitcases in the front hall, stuffed to overflowing.

His dad came around the corner from the kitchen and stopped. He was wearing his shoes.

"Oh . . . ," he said. "Morning, Eric."

"Morning," Eric said slowly. "Where you going?"

His father seemed to think about that for a moment. "Away for a while."

"Where?"

"Across the state. I . . . uh . . . I've got a place to stay there."

Eric frowned. "Why are you leaving now? What did Mom say?"

His dad stuffed his hands in his pockets. "She . . . uh . . . she doesn't know, Eric. I left a note."

"When are you coming back?"

"I don't know. I'll call. I left a note there . . . your mom can talk to you. It's going to be fine. You can watch yourself for a little bit, right? She'll be home just after four, like always."

He opened the door and then grabbed a suitcase in each hand. He forced a smile.

"It'll be fine. I'm just leaving for a bit. For work, you know? It's not a big deal."

"Oh . . . ," Eric said. "Okay. So . . . I'll see you soon then?"

"Yeah. A few weeks or so. Go back to bed. Sleep in. See you, bud."

He heaved the bags through the door and headed for his truck. Eric watched as he loaded them in the back, climbed in, and pulled out of the driveway much faster than usual. He gave Eric a wave and then quickly drove off. Eric never saw him again.

He absently played with a potato leaf as he remembered that night. His mom crying and screaming over the phone. Even then, Eric didn't *really* get it. It was weeks before he realized that his father wasn't coming back. After that, he stopped talking to the other kids. He had never been popular, but he had still tried. He had wanted to be accepted. But the day he realized that his dad had abandoned them was the same day he realized that being alone was the safest option. His mom was the one and only exception. He looked around the forest, thinking about her.

Maybe being alone was best for his mom too. She would think he had died in the earthquake, and she would mourn him for a while, and then she would move on. It was sad to picture her with a new family . . . but maybe it was for the best. Eric stared down at the potatoes. He could easily build a house in here—just to keep out the animals, since he wouldn't have to worry about the weather. There was lots of food and water and even light. He could stay.

But he couldn't get rid of the image of his mom crying. He

wasn't sure he could make her go through that. She'd already had to cry so much in the last few years.

Eric threw the potato leaf away. It was tempting, but at the very least she deserved to know he was alive. If he wanted to come back later, the forest wasn't going anywhere. For now, he had to keep moving.

Eric climbed to his feet and kept walking, pushing through the vines. The forest seemed to thin ahead, and he hurried forward, wondering if he had found the end. The trees suddenly fell away, and he stepped into some sort of clearing. A pool of clear water lay in the middle.

I would even have drinking water close by, he mused.

Eric shone his light across the water, and it fell on the far bank. There, standing as still as the trees, was a boy.

Seven and a Half Hours After

"HE HAD TO GO TO THE BATHROOM," SHANNON SAID, her voice shaking. "He just stepped to the side of the tunnel for a second and asked me to wait for him. I did, but I didn't hear anything for a bit. I called for him, and when I turned back, he was gone. Just like that. He vanished!"

The class pulled together behind Silvia, their flashlights darting around the chamber.

"It's okay," Tom said, his voice wavering just a bit. "I'm sure he just got lost. Brian!"

Shouts of *Brian!* echoed through the caverns, but there was no reply. Silvia started up the tunnel, shining her light into the darkness. There was nothing there. Brian really was gone.

She felt the bubble of fear in her stomach growing bigger. It was starting to choke her.

"I told you," Shannon sobbed. "Why would he walk off? Something got him!"

"What got him?" Marta asked. "There is nothing down here!"

"Monsters," Jordan said, looking at the tunnel and speaking at a near whisper.

"What kind of monsters?" Ashley said, sounding panicked.

Jordan gestured at the chamber. "Who knows? Look around you!"

"Giant bats, maybe," Greg said, checking the pockmarked chamber ceiling.

"We already saw a giant centipede," Derek said. "Maybe everything down here is big!"

"We're all going to be eaten," Naj murmured, stepping closer to the group.

The group pressed their backs together like a herd of elephants protecting their young, their flashlights shining wildly outward.

Silvia had seen enough. She was afraid too. But they needed to move.

"Are we going to look for Brian," she said loudly, "or just stand here?"

Silence greeted her, and then Tom nodded. "You're right. We have to find Brian."

Slowly, reluctantly, the class spread out again, and Silvia turned back to the tunnel. She wanted to curl up and cry. She wanted to run. She wanted to go home. But she couldn't do any of those things.

"Everyone stay close," she said, keeping her voice steady. "And keep your eyes open."

The tunnel sloped downward, and Silvia tried not to think about the fact that they were again descending deeper into the Earth. Why would Brian go down here? Had some giant animal really taken him? It seemed impossible. But everything down here did. Even her own actions.

Some days she could hardly get out of bed, she was so anxious. It was those days that the fear took over, and her breathing was short and her stomach hurt and she felt like she was going to shrivel up and die. And yet here she was leading a rescue operation. Where had that frightened, fragile girl gone? Why couldn't she always be like this one?

She didn't have the answer.

An hour seemed to crawl by to the soundtrack of a constant echoing *Brian!* and the scraping of shoes on the rock. Voices had eventually fallen to whispers and then gone silent, and still they made their way through the twisting, jagged passageways here— sometimes crouching and falling into single file as the tunnels grew smaller and smaller. Silvia began to feel like an ant. But she was still in the lead, and she picked one tunnel after another, never really knowing why.

Blisters had started to form on her heels—first as a stabbing pain and then just a gnawing, dull ache that made every step a chore. The unforgiving terrain was beginning to take its toll. She could hear people muttering behind her and wondered if they should stop for a break or give up the search altogether. It seemed like the tunnels were truly endless: up, down, left, right, and ultimately going nowhere.

As they approached two hours of searching, she heard a wrapper crackling behind her.

"Are you going to eat that whole thing?" Jordan suddenly asked.

Silvia glanced back to see a surprised Naj look up. "Yeah. Why?"

Jordan frowned. "Well, if we're going to walk across the entire country underground, we may want to start being a little smarter about our food. You know, like not eating everything."

"It's my granola bar," Naj said indignantly. "I can do what I want."

The whole group had come to a stop now, watching the exchange.

Jordan shrugged. "You can . . . but what happens when we run out of food? You going to eat mine? I don't think so. If we're going to survive as a group, we'd better start thinking like one."

Silvia stepped in between them. "We're not going to run out."

"Says who?" Jordan asked angrily. He pulled the map out of his pocket. "We're not anywhere near the original caverns. How can we be? We've been walking for hours. We could be down here for days at this rate. Weeks. How much food do we have left? Let's take another count. I've seen people snacking the whole time, not even thinking, while I sit here and ration."

"Fine," Silvia said. "Have we really eaten that much? What do we have left?"

Everyone opened their bags. They had consumed five granola bars, six juice boxes, ten water bottles, one Gatorade, two bananas, and a chocolate bar. People had been eating and drinking freely, and it had only been about ten hours by Silvia's count. Silvia frowned. They had barely a quarter of their original supplies left.

"Yeah," Jordan said, seeing her expression. "That's what I thought."

"Well, we have water," Silvia pointed out. "It's everywhere down here."

"Stagnant water," Jordan said. "It might need to be boiled, and we don't have a pot."

"So what are you suggesting?" Tom said.

"Someone should be put in charge of the food," Jordan said, folding his arms.

Naj shook his head. "Everyone should have their own."

"I don't have any food left," Ashley said. "What about me?"

"That's not my fault," Naj said defensively. "You should have packed more."

There was some muttering around the group as everyone took stock of their own food. A few people had nothing left, while those who did quickly put it back in their bags, looking protective. Silvia could feel the tension rising. Who would share food when it came down to it? She had a granola bar and an apple left. Would *she* share them?

Silvia considered Jordan's proposal. "I guess we could pool the food."

"Who would hold it?" Leonard asked suspiciously.

"I'll take it," Jordan said, opening his backpack and holding it out like a donations tray. "I don't mind carrying the extra weight, and I don't need to eat fifty grams of protein a day to make myself a better hockey player. No offense," he added, looking at Tom.

"None taken," Tom said dryly. "Well . . . maybe it's for the best."

There was more grumbling, but slowly everyone piled the remaining food into Jordan's bag. When they turned to Silvia, she reluctantly put her apple and granola bar in there as well.

"There," Jordan said, throwing the bag over his shoulders. "Now we can ration."

"When can we eat next?" Joanne asked, already looking longingly at his bag.

Jordan checked his watch. "It's been ten hours. At fourteen we'll have a bite."

"Agreed," Silvia said. "Let's keep moving."

She took the lead again and pushed on, but she was worried. If they didn't get out of here soon, there was going to be trouble. They had read *Lord of the Flies* in class at the beginning of the year. Things could get ugly very quickly.

Of course, they had more pressing problems than food. Was there really something living down here in the caverns big enough to take Brian? Or potentially even more scary . . . *someone?*

She thought about the M she had seen written on the wall with that chalky paste. Everyone else seemed to think it was a natural occurrence. She was really doubting that now.

Silvia was still thinking about that when she took a left turn, following the tunnel, and walked right into something sticky.

She tried to lift her flashlight but couldn't. She was stuck.

"What the heck?" she muttered.

The group turned the corner, and their flashlights suddenly fell on her. Silvia realized with horror that she was caught in a massive web of thick, black strands, like stretched tar. Then she looked up and froze. Eight beady eyes were staring back at her.

Eight Hours After

CARLOS STOOD AS RIGID AS STONE, HIS EYES locked on the brilliant white light and the strange boy holding it, nothing more than a silhouette behind the glow. His great-grandfather had been right: These people were demons and sorcerers. The glare stung his eyes, but he couldn't look away. He was staring at a living nightmare.

His grandmother had told him a story once, passed down from her mother before her. His grandmother was a wizened, shrunken woman, her hair a stark white and her hands like worn leather. Though it was only Kings who ruled in the Midnight Realm, she was deeply respected.

"Where did they come from?" Carlos had asked her, sitting cross-legged before the hearth.

His grandmother had stared up at the pressing darkness in the hall, her dark eyes clouded.

"They first came across the sea in great ships of wood. Ah, my father told me much about the sea. He went there once as a boy, before the descent into the dark. Endless water, mighty waves, and the cries of birds and sailors and great monsters in the deep. The Mother does not dare go there."

Carlos had shivered at the thought. If the Mother was afraid, it must be a terrible place.

"They spread across the lands, killing all who stood in their way. Our people were attacked on two sides: the Spanish on one, and the English on the other. Many of our people died in the great wars. Other native peoples were slain too—none could stand against the invaders."

"Why?" Carlos said, sitting up on his haunches. "Why couldn't they beat them?"

His grandmother had looked down at him. "The invaders were too strong. Their weapons were greater, their numbers large. Weapons of terrible noise and invisible death. They are demons, Carlos. Even many years later, the fighting continued. The invaders had long ago won the war, but they still came for our land. When they came to my father's village, his people rose up. Many were killed, including his parents. But my father managed to push the invaders back, just for a few days. In that time, he rounded up the rest of the village and led them here."

Carlos's grandmother had smiled, and her eyes drifted again as if seeing her dead father.

"For his heroism they named him King, the first of your line.

But I tell you this, Carlos, the demons are still up there. We must be vigilant. If they come for us, we will all die."

And now the day had come. All the fears and whispers and grim stories were true.

His hand slowly moved to the sword hilt jutting out over his right shoulder, his eyes still locked on the demon. Would the surface boy kill him before he could draw his sword? Was that strange white light some sort of magic weapon? Perhaps he should run and return with soldiers.

No. I cannot just leave him here in this place. I cannot flee before the Mother.

His hand closed on the hilt, the smooth, cool bone comforting against his fingers. His heart was pounding, his stomach tight with fear. But there was no choice, and he prepared to launch himself around the pool in a desperate attack. He had to protect the Mother in this sacred place, and the boy sorcerer had to die before he could destroy the Midnight Realm.

"Hello?" the boy called. "Who's there?"

Carlos stiffened at the voice, confused, and his hand fell away from the hilt. The boy spoke their language. His accent was a bit different—harsher, perhaps—but the words were clear. Carlos's father and grandmother had never mentioned anything about that—they both just said they were cruel savages. Perhaps this boy was not from the surface after all.

"Who are you?" Carlos called back, squinting against the light.

For the first time, he noticed how beautiful the still water appeared in the glare. The surface glittered like diamonds, and the light pierced into the depths. He looked at it in wonder.

"My name is Eric Johnson," the boy replied. "I'm lost down here. Who are you?"

Carlos paused. But he could see no reason to lie about his name.

"My name is Carlos Santi. How did you find this place?"

"We fell in the earthquake . . . my class and me. I don't know where they are."

"You are alone?" Carlos asked, his eyes darting around the forest edge.

"Yes."

Carlos relaxed just a little and let his hand fall to his side. He had been afraid the others were close behind. Even so, the boy could be lying. If he was a demon, then he might try to lure Carlos into a trap. Perhaps the light would freeze him somehow. Carlos kept a hand by his knife.

"Can I come around?" Eric asked.

"Yes," Carlos said warily. "But leave your weapons."

"I don't have any weapons."

Carlos frowned. "What is that light then?"

"It's a cell phone. Here." The light suddenly flicked out again, returning the forest to its comforting blue glow. The boy hesitated. "Can you leave *your* weapons, though? The knife and sword—maybe leave those over there? We'll meet at the side of the pond."

Carlos ran a hand over his knife. The boy seemed innocent enough.

"Fine," Carlos said. "Move slowly."

Carlos laid down his sword and knife on the bank, his skin prickling as he stepped away. Was this all a trick? He remembered something his father had once told him.

The invaders came with promises, he said. *But they only ever brought death.*

Carlos gingerly rounded the pool, hoping the Mother was watching over him. Eric moved just as slowly. Without the stinging glare in his eyes, Carlos could get a much better look at him.

Eric was slender and tall, with dark skin and curly black hair—not at all like the white, bearded men Juarez the First had described. Eric moved tentatively, and he looked afraid.

As they finally came face to face, Carlos could see his clothes clearly as well, and he could not hide his fascination. Eric wore dark blue pants and a black, long-sleeve shirt, both made of curious fabrics he had never seen. On his feet were crisp white shoes tied with thin rope.

At the same time as Carlos was puzzling over the boy's clothes, he saw Eric scanning his attire, and he seemed just as surprised by it. The two met eyes, and Carlos held his gaze until Eric turned away, wondering if this boy was truly a savage. It did not seem like it.

"You speak the same language," Carlos said.

Eric frowned. "Yeah . . . English. Where are you from, Carlos?"

"English . . . that's what you call it?"

Eric looked even more confused. "Yes. What do you call it?"

"The King's tongue," Carlos said. "I . . . I thought it was only used here."

Eric stared at him for a long time, focusing on his rat-hide boots. Finally, he looked up.

"Where are you from?" he repeated softly.

Carlos approved of the boy's voice, at least. He was appropriately quiet and respectful.

"I live nearby," he said, unwilling to reveal anything specific about his people.

Eric ran a trembling hand through his hair. "You . . . you live down here in the caves? For how long? How? How did you get here?"

"I have always lived here."

Eric looked like he was in shock. "But how . . . how is that possible—"

"How many of you are there?" Carlos asked.

"Fourteen students. One teacher . . . Mr. Baker. But I don't know where they are. I don't even know if the other students are okay. . . ."

"They have been spotted," Carlos said. "They are alive."

Eric slumped in relief. "Where are they?"

Carlos weighed his options. If the boy was truly lost down here, he could help Carlos find the others and get them all out of the Realm again. Perhaps the surface humans only became savage when they were older. . . . Eric *seemed* fine. It was risky, but they needed to move quickly.

"I don't know," Carlos said. "But we need to find them before the Worms do."

"The . . . the what?" Eric asked.

"The Worms. They are exiles from my people. I cannot let them get your weapons."

"We don't have—"

"Whatever you call them. These lights. Your clothes and shoes. They will take them."

Eric nervously looked out at the woods. "These . . . Worms. Are they dangerous?"

Carlos nodded and went to retrieve his weapons. "The Worms are like animals, savage and wild. If they find your friends, they will kill them all. So we had better find them first."

Ten Hours After

SILVIA STARED UP AT THE GLINTING EYES, UNABLE TO move or scream or do anything but watch the creature's deadly, methodical approach. As the spider emerged fully into the light, gnashing two curved black fangs, she felt her knees fail her, and her entire body went limp into the web.

The spider was the size of a small car, and its head and legs were covered with a thick mat of hair some six inches long. Its body was slate gray, except for a huge black triangle on its bulbous abdomen. But the worst of all were the fangs—each at least a foot long.

For a second, it seemed as if no one could move. Silvia just stared up at the monster, still hanging there like a stunned dragonfly. Then her mind suddenly flared back to life, pumping her with the pounding fears and anxieties and desperation that it sometimes did for no reason at all.

But this time it was welcome.

Silvia thrashed against the web, freeing her right hand just enough to shine the flashlight right into the spider's face. It recoiled, turning its head.

"Help me!" she shouted.

The class finally snapped out of their daze. Tom, Shannon, and Jordan rushed forward, each grabbing one of her limbs and tugging. The web was incredibly strong. Silvia looked up and saw the massive spider slowly turning back toward her, its eyes adjusting to the light.

Tom followed her gaze. "Uh oh," he said weakly.

"Faster!" Silvia shrieked.

Naj rushed forward, followed by Mary and Marta. Above, the spider took another slow step toward them, gnashing its twin fangs. Silvia waved the flashlight at it in warning.

Tom and Shannon grabbed her snagged arm, and Jordan took a leg. Mary and Marta grabbed her other leg, while Naj wrapped his arms around her waist and tried to brace his feet.

"Any time now," Silvia said, as the fangs came within a few feet of her head.

Poison glistened on the tips—clear and acidic. A large droplet started to form.

"On three," Jordan said, taking a fistful of her jeans. "One, two . . ."

"Now!" Silvia shouted, as the spider lunged.

They pulled as hard as they could. The web stretched and then broke, and all seven of them tumbled backward just as the glistening fangs bit into empty air. The spider released a hiss, eyeing the group as they lay sprawled on top of one another—vulnerable.

The rest of the class finally rushed forward, pointing their flashlights at the spider, and Silvia felt many arms help her to her feet. As the spider continued to hiss, the flashlights landed on another pair of eight eyes behind it. And then another. The spiders were everywhere.

"Run!" Silvia shouted, helping Naj up and then racing down an adjoining tunnel.

The narrow tunnel sloped downward almost immediately, but no one cared. She heard the rest of the class barreling down the passage behind her as their hysterical shouts echoed through the caverns. Silvia continued to lead the way farther and farther down, the flashlight bobbing ahead of her and falling on one obstacle after another. Dodge around a stalagmite, climb a boulder, jump over a crevice.

She screamed warnings about each one, and she didn't hear anyone stumble or fall.

The tunnel took a final turn downward, almost causing her to slip, and then she ran out into another open chamber. The rest of the group emerged behind her, gasping for breath. Naj looked like he was ready to pass out, and he dropped onto the floor, grabbing his cramping sides.

"Not cool," he managed.

"Did they follow us?" Greg asked in a panic.

"No," Joanne said, who had come in last. "They stayed with their webs."

Silvia did a quick head count and saw that everyone was

there and accounted for. Derek and Leonard were pacing back and forth with their hands on their heads, looking almost manic.

"Did you see that, bro?"

"Of course I saw it! It must have weighed a metric ton!"

"It was huge! Not a ton though."

"Are you blind, dude? It might have been two. Each fang was probably twenty pounds."

"What do you think they were made of, lead?"

Silvia wiped her face and then pulled Ashley, who was completely white, into a hug.

"I'm . . . I'm sorry," Ashley said.

Silvia frowned and pulled back. "Why?"

"I didn't help you. I froze. I didn't know what to do."

Silvia hugged her again. "I don't blame you. I froze myself."

"Sil . . . ," Jordan said, "you might want to look at this."

Silvia turned around and followed his trembling finger. "Oh . . ."

In front of them was another underground lake, still and black and stretching off to the far side of the chamber where another wall was just visible at the edge of their flashlights, maybe fifty yards away. The lake stretched to both side walls as well, blocking their way forward.

But far stranger was the small patch of forest that stretched around the bank to their right.

There were trees, though they were old and bent and covered with vines and brambles like dusty drapery. Yellow and green shrubs packed the ground between them to create a thick undergrowth. Great multicolored mushrooms stood taller than the trees, while smaller, glowing ones covered the ground, lighting the forest like blue spotlights.

Tom stepped up beside her. "Am I seeing this correctly?" he muttered.

"I don't know," Silvia replied. "What you're seeing is supposed to be impossible."

"Fascinating," Naj said, looking like he was eager to go explore the trees.

Tom shook his head and took a deep drink of water, almost finishing his bottle.

"You'd better watch how much you drink," Jordan said.

He was in charge of the food, but the water and Gatorade had been left to each individual's discretion. And they were all drinking fast.

"There's water everywhere," Tom said, giving him a dirty look.

"Water that might be poison for all you know," Jordan retorted.

The two boys stared each other down again, posturing.

"I'll take my chances," Tom said, and then he chugged the rest of his water.

At that, a few others seemed convinced enough to drink their own bottles. Leonard chugged his, wiping his mouth and sighing, and Joanne and Naj did the same. Silvia decided to hold off on hers. She took a little sip and tucked the bottle away again. She would at least fill it with running water from a river or stream.

Silvia shined her flashlight in either direction, but there was no way around the lake, and there were no more openings on this bank. She thought she could see one on the other side, however.

They had to either go back up the tunnel, or swim across the lake.

"We can't go back," Tom reasoned. "We'd have to go past the spiders."

Silvia nodded. "But do we really want to get in the lake?"

Tom looked out at the black water. "Not really. Let's go talk to the group."

Many of the students were repacking their bags and staring grimly out at the water.

Silvia hesitated. "It looks like we're going to have to cross the lake."

"We're going to swim across?" Leonard asked, incredulous. "No . . . let's go back."

"I am not going back to those spiders," Joanne said flatly. "No way."

"What if we just sit and wait?" Mary suggested, huddling in the middle of the group with her sister. "Like Jordan said. I mean, we tried to walk and it didn't work so let's stop moving."

Jordan nodded. "Finally, someone else sees some reason."

Silvia shook her head. "For what? A magical rescue team to find us? We went over this before. They don't even know these parts of the caverns exist. They may *never* find us here. And so what then? We sit here until we run out of food? What happens when we all start starving?"

That hung over the group for a moment. Even Jordan looked downcast at the thought.

"We have to cross the lake," Silvia said firmly. "No one will find us here, and I am going home. If you want to stay, I can't stop you."

"We don't know what's in that water!" Leonard said.

"We were already in a lake," Tom said. "We survived that."

"Mr. Baker didn't," Joanne pointed out softly.

Silvia turned back to the woods, thinking about poor Mr. Baker. He had been so excited about this trip. What would he do if he was here? He would be optimistic, she was sure of that. And he would also tell them to be creative. To think their way out of the problem.

Her eyes fell on the forest.

"We need to cross," she said. "But maybe we can at least make it a little easier."

"Like a raft?" Tom said, following her gaze.

"Exactly," she said. "Or at least something we can hold onto."

"I would like that," Shannon said. "I'm not a really good swimmer."

"It won't help you if a monster decides to eat you," Leonard muttered.

"Len," Tom said warningly. "Come on. We don't have a choice. Let's go."

Silvia nodded and started for the woods. Jordan, Tom, and a few others caught up to her, and everyone looked at the thicket worriedly as they approached. Ashley stayed close behind Silvia, obviously not wanting to get too close to the shadowy forest. No one did.

"Are you sure about this?" Ashley whispered.

"No," Silvia admitted. "But it's the best plan I can think of."

She reached the woods and looked up at a huge, rounded

white mushroom. It was as tall as her garage, and it looked ghostly and pale in the flashlights, like an ancient dinosaur bone.

"That is a large mushroom," Ashley muttered, shining her light on the crimson cap.

Silvia stepped forward to try and break off some of the smaller fungi and branches, wondering if she could lash them together with the vines. She grabbed a strange, leafy brown plant and snapped the thin stalk in two, letting cool droplets of water spill out over her hands.

"Silvia . . . ," Ashley's voice was trembling.

"Yeah?" Silvia replied, glancing back at her distractedly.

"You might want to step out of the woods."

Silvia frowned. "What is it?"

Ashley pointed a shaking finger upward. Silvia turned and looked up at the canopy, where Ashley's flashlight was illuminating small, glittering eyes. Hundreds of them.

Suddenly a shrill cry tore through the air like a knife, and the forest came alive.

Twelve and a Half Hours After

ERIC STAYED A FEW FEET BEHIND THE SWIFT-MOVING Carlos, though he noticed the boy constantly checked back on him. He deliberately left his cell light off, knowing Carlos was wary of it, and instead relied on the eerie blue light of the fungi. He felt clumsy compared to Carlos, who seemed to glide through the forest as if barely touching the ground. His feet deftly avoided branches and holes.

Eric was getting tired. He didn't want to admit it, but his sides were burning with cramp. He was also burning with curiosity.

"So . . . how long have your people been down here?" he asked.

Carlos sidestepped a large mushroom, slicing a piece off as he did and drinking from it. Eric watched in amazement. The mushroom was like a desert cactus, storing the water.

"Over a hundred years," he finally replied.

Eric shook his head in amazement. "But . . . where did you come from?"

Carlos glanced back at him. "The first Midnight King came from the surface. Juarez the First. He came to escape the people there. Your people . . . I suppose."

A tiny bit of venom had crept into his voice.

Eric frowned. "My people? It was over a hundred years ago."

"We are our father's blood, are we not?"

Eric snorted. "I hope we're more than that."

Carlos looked at Eric as if he had said something particularly odd, but he didn't respond. He pushed ahead faster, stepping over a small running stream that was bristling with tiny reeds. Eric fell back a little, trying to keep up with one hand on his side, squeezing the aching cramp.

Finally, the shrunken old trees thinned and began to fall away. Carlos stepped onto open ground, and Eric came out after him, bending over to catch his breath. His eyes stung with sweat.

"We will take a break," Carlos said, eyeing him.

"Cool," Eric managed.

He plunked onto the ground and took a deep drink of his water. Carlos snapped off one of the bioluminescent fungi at its base and dropped it in front of them, forming a bizarre blue campfire. Then he broke a branch off one of the gnarled old trees, sat down crossed-legged directly across from Eric, and began to chew on it. Eric watched him in fascination.

"What is that?"

Carlos looked up, then snapped off the bottom and threw it to him. "Barbar tree."

Eric caught the branch and began to gnaw on it. It was bitter, but it had a rich, earthy taste as well, like when his dad had once let him try a piece of truffle. As he bit deeper into the branch, the taste grew a little sweeter, and he smiled at Carlos.

"It's good," he said.

Carlos looked surprised. "Not many people like it."

"I like this kind of stuff," Eric said. "I'm used to eating things out in the wild."

He dug into his backpack. Carlos tensed, his hand dropping down to his knife, but Eric quickly pulled out a granola bar and showed it to him.

Too bad it's raisin, he thought.

He slowly unwrapped it, aware that Carlos was still sitting very upright, and then broke a piece off for himself, taking a bite. He handed the granola bar to Carlos, who accepted it warily.

"What is it?" he asked.

"Try it."

Carlos sniffed it, and then took a bite. His face immediately lit up. "Delicious."

Eric laughed and waved for him to take it. "We'll trade then. It's not my favorite."

Suddenly all his concerns about food and water were gone. If Carlos and his people had lived down here for a hundred years, there was obviously plenty of both.

"Tell me more about these Worms," Eric said.

Carlos's smile slipped away. "They are led by an evil woman named Jana. No . . . a girl, I suppose. She is sixteen. Her mother died when she was young from a sickness, her father was executed for treason, and her brother for poaching on the King's Land."

"She doesn't sound evil to me," Eric said.

Carlos took another bite of the granola bar, chewing it slowly with his eyes closed.

"She wasn't at first, perhaps. When her father was executed, his family was exiled to the Worm Lands: Jana, her brother, and her aunt and cousins. My great-grandfather said if there is treason in the blood, it must be quelled. All the Worms are outcasts from my people—if one goes, they bring their family with them. The Worms live in the outreaches of the Realm, scavenging rats and insects and whatever else they can find. But they were never violent before."

He put the granola bar down, his eyes now on the glowing mushroom.

"When Jana got to the Worm Lands, she changed things. They had always stayed in their own lands, but Jana took over and declared war. Her father was killed in a most . . . unpleasant way, and she wanted vengeance. They became like shadows, and we could not find them. She murdered one of my soldiers and took another hostage, eventually returning him just so he could deliver a message: that she intended to kill the King and end the line. Jana started calling herself the Shadow Queen. The war escalated, and more have died."

Eric looked around nervously. The mushroom cast only a ten-foot radius of light at best. Anyone could be out there.

Carlos sighed. "I did not wish for this war. There was a century of peace before this."

"And they would harm my friends?" Eric asked nervously.

"I believe so," Carlos said. "They are as vicious and deceitful as rats."

Eric sat back, taking another sip of water and staring at the glowing forest.

"I was just about to tell you how much I like it down here," he said ruefully.

"You do?"

Eric nodded. "It's quiet. You can live off the land and without anyone's help."

"You should see my village on Descent Day. There is song and dance and food."

"That's not what I want," Eric replied, shaking his head. "I want to be alone."

Carlos stared at him for a moment, chewing on the last of the granola bar. "You do not like your people?"

"They don't like me," Eric said quietly.

Carlos frowned and climbed back to his feet, scooping up the mushroom and throwing it back in the woods, where it crashed into the undergrowth. "Come. We must get moving again."

"One second," Eric said.

He flicked on his light and pulled out his notepad, finishing the circle of the forest now that he was out of it and marking the

pool where he had met Carlos. He wrote a small note as well, and
Carlos walked over to look.

"What do you think?" Eric said.

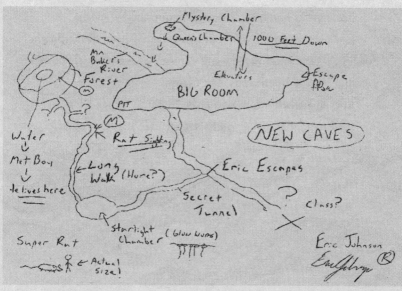

Carlos looked it over carefully, slowly tracing his hand along
the river.

"So that is how you came. I have not been to what you call the
Big Room, or the Mystery Room. I do not know these 'elevators' or
this escape you speak of with the funny picture. But that river you
drew is the very lifeblood of my people. It is not a bad map. But you
have turned, and you are heading back along the river now—farther
from the escape. This class . . . that is the others you were with?"

"Yes."

He nodded. "Good. We will follow the river. And we will fix
your map later."

Carlos extended a hand and helped Eric to his feet.

"A Super Rat?" Carlos said, smiling. "I like that. My sister would like your pictures."

Eric put his notebook away. "What do the Ms mean?"

Carlos started walking. "It means you are within the Midnight Realm . . . the land of the King. Those Ms were put there as a reminder of our boundaries. The Worms are banned there."

Eric hurried after him anxiously. "Is he . . . a nice King?"

Carlos laughed. "You will have to decide that for yourself."

Thirteen Hours After

SILVIA SPILLED BACKWARD, HITTING HER TAILBONE
hard on the ground as a wave of screeching shapes erupted from
the trees. She gasped and rolled onto her side, covering her head
as the tide of black swept overhead.

Bats, she thought. *They're just bats.*

She looked up and saw Ashley screaming and running—but
not before flinging her flashlight away and letting it smash onto
the ground. She fell into darkness and screamed louder.

Silvia climbed to her feet and pointed her light at the plume
of bats spiraling toward the cavern ceiling. It was strangely beautiful, like a shoal of tiny fish twisting into a massive bait ball.

Around her, the rest of the class was either running or flatten-
ing themselves against the floor, crying out. The cavern echoed
with so much noise it was as if they were caught in a thunder-
storm: flapping and sobbing and worst of all, the occasional
sound of a smashing light.

"It's just bats!" she called, but she doubted anyone could hear her.

Finally, the last of the bats swept upward toward the cavern ceiling, disappearing into the blackness and leaving only their shrill, echoing cries. Silvia walked over and helped Ashley up. "Sorry," Ashley murmured, looking sheepishly at her shattered flashlight.

Silvia just shook her head, took out the batteries, and stuffed them into her pocket.

"Everyone all right?" Silvia asked, shining the cell light on each of them in turn.

Joanne, Tom, and Jordan nodded, though Tom was as white as the mushrooms.

"Just bats," Silvia said. "We're in a cave, right? Makes sense. Let's get back to work."

Using their remaining lights, they managed to collect a large bushel of branches and fungi, spreading them out into three piles on the cavern floors. Leonard and Derek—who had both seemed a little embarrassed after screaming and running away from the bats—had taken the lead in designing the small rafts. Silvia had wanted one large one, but they thought it was impractical.

"It's really a matter of structural integrity," Leonard was saying, examining one pile. "The larger the raft, the sturdier it has to be."

"Can't we just throw this all in the lake and swim with it?" Ashley asked dryly.

Derek looked shocked. "Without creating dry spots for our bags? No measurements?"

"Just do your thing," Silvia said, running her fingers along one of the trees curiously.

"I'm thinking three large mushroom stalks with smaller branches running perpendicular across. We then wrap each junction with the vines," Leonard said. "Simple physics, baby."

"We could do that . . . if we wanted to sink," Derek retorted.

Silvia ignored the ensuing argument, stepping into the woods. She knelt and examined some of the holes on the ground, and grinned as a small yellow lizard scurried past.

"Hey, little guy," she said.

She spotted two more lizards, a large black beetle, and a scurrying rodent that was likely blind, until she heard Derek shout that they were finished.

Silvia emerged from the woods again to see that the class had created three rafts, each about the size of a computer desk. The tree branches had been lashed tightly together with vines.

"I give you the Santa Maria, Pinta, and Nina," Leonard said.

Silvia laughed. "Beautiful. Do they float?"

Leonard and Derek exchanged a look. "Well . . . we haven't tested that yet."

"I see," Silvia said dryly. "Well, maybe we should do that."

They dragged the small rafts to the water and pushed them in. They floated easily.

"Yeah, boyyy!" Leonard said, and he and Derek exchanged a high five.

"Ridgewood mathletes whaaaaaat?" Tom whooped. His voice echoed through the chamber.

"Yes, yes, very impressive," Silvia said, trying to hold back a laugh. She turned to the group. "Everyone put your flashlights up on the rafts. We're down to five, so we have to be careful."

"Really careful," Jordan muttered.

Nobody moved, so Silvia stepped into the water first. The lake was frigid, and she felt the chill seep into her bones. She grabbed the smallest raft, putting her bag on top of it.

"Pleasant," she said, her teeth chattering.

Ashley stepped in after her, and then Tom grabbed the far end, both piling their bags next to hers.

"Here goes nothing," he said.

The three of them pushed the raft into deeper water. Silvia gasped as the air rushed out of her and the lake crept under her clothes. She shivered violently as she started to kick underwater.

"What happened to . . . to . . . volcanic springs?" Ashley managed.

"Come on!" Silvia called behind her, and she heard the others pushing into the water.

"What is this, the Arctic Circle?" Naj cried out.

"I can't feel my feet," Leonard moaned.

"I told you we should have designed seats and paddles!" Derek added.

As the shore dwindled behind them, so did the light. Silvia had positioned hers to point straight ahead, but it bobbled a little until it was pointing sideways at a bag. The darkness rushed back in, and the groups behind her seemed to be having the same problem. Her hearing and smell seemed to sharpen in the darkness, until she could pick out the sounds of each kicking leg, the bizarre, earthy smell of their mushroom raft, and a hint of sulfur, like rotting eggs.

"I th-th-think I'm good with caves for a while," Tom said.

"Yeah," Ashley said, sounding relieved someone had spoken. "I'm good w-with Albuquerque. A hotel and a play or t-two sound half decent right now. Or home, maybe."

Silvia forced a laugh. "What's the f-first thing you want to do when you get out?"

"Eat p-p-pizza and watch some N-Netflix," Tom said through the chattering.

"Same," Silvia said longingly.

She thought of watching TV with her parents, and how that seemed lame just a few days ago. They had movie nights on Sundays, and her mom would make popcorn in the pot so that it came out fresh and steaming and drizzled with butter. She could almost taste the rich saltiness.

They had done Sunday movie nights since she was a kid. Only once was it cancelled.

She had been midway through the movie when she choked on a piece of a popcorn. No . . . not choked. It was just a little kernel really . . . more of a tickle than anything else. But she started to panic, and her skin flushed, and before she knew it she was sweating and even a drink didn't make her feel better. She felt like she couldn't breathe, and she excused herself to the bathroom.

That was when a panic attack struck. Soon she was huddled on the floor, crying and gasping and grabbing her chest until her mom was holding her. They went to the doctor for the first time the next day, and he said it was just a freak occurrence. Her dad liked that explanation.

But there were more attacks, and she didn't eat popcorn anymore.

Silvia thought about that as she pushed through the still water. It seemed so long ago.

"So," Tom said, "h-how do you feel about s-s-swimming?"

Silvia laughed, letting the ridiculousness of the moment sink in. Ashley joined in.

"Love it," Silvia said. "I just w-won't ever do it again. Maybe boating—"

"Wait," Tom said quietly. "Did you f-feel that?"

Silvia fell quiet. And then she felt it. It wasn't much, just a gentle current against her leg. A subtle change in the water. And then another current swept past, pulling at her legs.

"What is that?" Ashley whispered.

"I d-don't know," Silvia said. "But I d-d-doubt it's something good. Swim faster!"

"Agreed!" Tom said.

"Pick up the pace!" Silvia called back. "Let's g-go!"

The words were barely out of her mouth when the water moved again, stronger this time. Silvia looked down just as a massive, translucent white head swam below her dangling feet.

Thirteen and a Half Hours After

CARLOS KEPT THEM MOVING QUICKLY, THOUGH HE knew Eric was struggling to keep up. He felt guilty for pushing him so hard, but every moment that passed was another that the Worms could find the other surface humans. Eric seemed to understand that, and despite his obvious discomfort, he did not complain.

Carlos glanced back at Eric, conflicted. He didn't want to admit it, but he almost liked him. He was soft-spoken and determined and seemed to respect the Midnight Realm. None of it matched the stories, but he was still nervous. His father would never approve.

Carlos dodged around a rocky outcropping—just a darker shade of black.

"A foot to your right," he said quietly.

His warnings were the only direction Eric had. Carlos knew he would have liked to use his white light, but it would have been much too visible in the darkness. If the Worms spotted them, they would become the hunted very quickly. He liked Eric, but he didn't look like much of a fighter, unless he did have weapons. Eric followed, avoiding the rock. He was breathing heavily.

Carlos tried to slow down just a little, leading them around a corner.

"Turn right slowly," he said.

"This is crazy," Eric muttered. "I'm walking blind."

"You're doing well."

Carlos had his eyes trained ahead, but his mind was preoccupied. He tried to think of where the other surface humans would go. Santiago had spotted them by the Black Lake, and he said they were on the move. Most of the tunnels in the area funneled into two large chambers. The Room of Light was possible, but the biggest chamber contained the Forbidden Lake. Carlos's people had avoided those freezing cold waters since the first days of the Realm. He hoped the surface humans wouldn't be foolish enough to cross there.

Still, it was a good starting place. He took a left at the next opening, leading them to the lake. Suddenly Eric cried out, shattering the watchful silence of the tunnel and spilling to the ground.

Carlos turned back and knelt beside him. "What's wrong?"

"My ankle," he managed, grabbing it. "I think I twisted it."

Carlos looked back and saw a crevice in the ground. He had walked over it without thinking. *"Haga,"* he swore. "I am sorry. Can you sit up again?"

He helped Eric up, and then gingerly pressed his ankle.

"Not broken," Carlos said, relieved. "Sprained, maybe. Hold still."

He reached into his pocket and pulled out folded yew leaves and slender, strong jori vines. He hoped they would be long enough to wrap the ankle securely.

"What are you doing?" Eric said, clearly in pain. "I can't see, remember?"

Carlos stayed still for a moment, listening for movement. "You can put your light on."

Eric pulled out what he called a cell phone and turned the light on, facing himself.

"I'm going to wrap the ankle," Carlos said. "Okay?"

Eric nodded, and Carlos slipped off his shoe and pulled the leaves tightly around his ankle, securing them with the vines. Eric grimaced, but he did not cry out.

"You said something earlier," Carlos said, tying the last vines. "You said you hoped we were more than the blood of our fathers. Why?"

Eric shrugged. "My father left a few years ago. I haven't seen him since."

"He left your family? Why would he do that?"

"To start a new one," Eric said, sounding bitter. "A family he liked more, I guess."

Carlos finished with the vines and sat back on his haunches. "I am sorry."

"Its fine," Eric said, gingerly pulling his shoe on. "He's a jerk."

Carlos stared at him for a moment. "I . . . we are supposed to be like our fathers."

"No thanks," Eric said. "I don't want to be anything like that guy. How is your dad?"

Carlos looked away. "He died."

"Sorry."

"He . . . he was a great man. Everyone says it. I have always tried to be like him."

Eric tested his ankle, wincing. "And how's that going for you?"

"It's not always easy," Carlos admitted. "I feel like I am failing him more than not."

"You know why?" Eric said.

Carlos turned to him, frowning. "Why?"

"Because you're not him," Eric said simply. "I spent a long time trying to be more like my dad, and it didn't work. It *doesn't* work, I think. I would just worry about being yourself."

He tried to stand, and Carlos helped him up. Soon they were standing eye to eye.

"It's not that easy," Carlos said. "People expect me to be like him."

Eric took a few careful steps. "People expect lots of things. I gave up on that a while ago." He turned back and grinned. "This stuff works pretty well. It feels like a brace."

"Good," Carlos said, thinking about Eric's words. No one spoke like that in the Realm. "Come on. Keep your light on . . . I will listen for any Worms. We don't need you falling again."

Eric nodded, and the two of them set off down the tunnel once more.

"I fear your friends may have gone to the Forbidden Lake," Carlos said.

"That sounds bad," Eric said weakly. "Why is it forbidden?"

Carlos paused. "There are things living in there. Big things."

Fourteen Hours After

SILVIA WATCHED WITH A MIXTURE OF HORROR AND fascination as the monstrous creature glided beneath them. It was at least twenty feet long and shaped like a whale, though it was also glowing brightly enough to illuminate the silhouette of her legs, and its tail floated out behind it like two dangling ribbons.

The creature swept right past their raft and then started to turn, as if preparing to circle back for them. It looked large enough to swallow them all in a single, gaping bite.

"What . . . what is that?" Ashley said, her voice cracking and weak.

"Swim!" Tom shouted.

Silvia started to kick furiously, taking one hand off the raft to paddle with that as well. She had never been a great swimmer, but now she pushed with everything she had. Ashley and Tom did the same, until the spray was kicking up over their heads and dripping down her face.

More and more screams filled the chamber as the rest of the class spotted the huge, luminescent sea creature, and Silvia heard frantic splashing and kicking as they started to panic.

"Just keep s-swimming!" she said loudly.

The creature continued to glide around them. The nightmarish race through the lake felt like hours, and she began to wonder if she had just imagined the shore on the other side. What if the lake stretched on for miles? What if they didn't make it?

Finally, when her arms and legs were burning with exhaustion, her foot kicked solid ground. She grabbed her bag and raced up the shore, Tom and Ashley close behind. Ashley flung herself onto the ground, crying, but Silvia quickly climbed onto a rock and perched there like a seagull, shining her flashlight back out over the lake for the others.

Nine terrified faces stared back at her, swimming and thrashing wildly. But that was all she could see. The water was dark again—the creature must have descended back into the deep.

"It's okay," she said, looking around the lake with her light. "It's gone."

Silvia considered the creature now that the panic had subsided. Truthfully, it had been incredibly beautiful. A shark species like the basking shark was more likely to thrive down here in the dark. She wondered if they would ever have the chance to tell anyone about the new species.

"The Spirit Shark," she whispered. She liked the sound of it.

Soon the class was ashore again, and they huddled together, shivering. Some began to wring out clothes or empty shoes, while others just stood there quietly. Silvia joined them.

"Let's take a break," she said. "Dry out and stuff. Jordan, how about some food?"

Jordan paused. "Yeah, we can have some snacks."

The class gathered around in a broken circle, taking off their shoes and letting the water splash out onto the rocks. Jordan began passing out morsels of food: granola bars and pieces of banana. Everyone dug into them hungrily. Silvia hadn't even realized how hungry she was.

"This is the best banana of my life," Naj said, savoring each bite.

Greg laughed. "I don't even like granola bars, but this is pretty good."

"I want pizza," Tom said longingly. "From Rico's."

"Why would you say that?" Ashley moaned. "That's all I can think about now."

"I am going to eat so much when we get home," Mary said. "Just TV and food. It's going to be amazing."

"I hope that's soon," Marta said. "I am so sick of this place."

Jordan was sitting cross-legged with his map. "You have to admit . . . it's kind of cool."

"Cool?" Derek asked incredulously.

"We're exploring a new world," Jordan said. "You don't get to do that often."

"I'll just stick to World of Warcraft, thanks," Naj said.

Shannon finished her piece of granola bar and sighed. "You know . . . I was worried about exams next week. Like . . . stressing about them. They seemed like the most important things ever."

"Well, they are forty percent of your grade," Jordan pointed out.

Shannon rolled her eyes. "The point is, they don't seem very important anymore."

"Think they'll be cancelled?" Mary asked hopefully.

"We don't know where our teacher is," Silvia said. "I think that's a bit of an issue." Silence fell over the class again, and Silvia felt a bit guilty. "But it's Mr. Baker we're talking about," she said. "Knowing him, he's probably skipping along taking plant samples on the other side of the caverns."

Everyone laughed.

"Definitely," Tom said. "He is loving this. And then he can tell everybody about it when we get out. No one is going to believe us."

"I'm not sure I do either," Silvia said, pushing back her sopping wet hair.

"Think we might be famous after this?" he asked.

Jordan snorted. "Either famous or dead."

Tom laughed. "Well, they seem to go hand in hand sometimes." He forlornly put his shoes back on, grimacing at the cold and wiping his runny nose. "No more swimming?"

"Agreed," Silvia said. "You think we should get moving or should we take a—"

She stopped when she saw the look on Tom's face.

Silvia slowly turned around. "What . . . ?" she whispered

Torches had suddenly flared to life behind them, illuminating a line of filthy men and women—ten in all. They were lean and muscular; the men had scraggly black beards and big eyes, while the women had long, knotted hair that spilled down past their waists and over clothes made of fur. There was only one with short hair, and she stood at the front—a teenager, with the darkest eyes Silvia had ever seen and a jagged knife in her hand.

The knife was held to Brian's throat, while her free arm was wrapped around his chest.

The girl looked at them, her eyes flashing in the lights.

"Do not move, surface demons, or this one will die."

Fourteen and a Half Hours After

THE TWO BOYS MOVED AS QUICKLY AS POSSIBLE through the maze of tunnels. Eric's ankle was still throbbing, but the wrap Carlos made allowed him to put weight on it without rolling it again. Carlos was clearly impatient to go faster. He kept hurrying ahead, glancing back, and returning.

"You can leave me behind, you know," Eric said.

Carlos shook his head. "No. It is too dangerous. The Worms could find you too."

"I don't understand," Eric said, slowly picking his way around a crevice. "Why don't you guys just invite these Worms to live with you again and end this whole war? It sounds like Jana is angry your people sent her family away and had her father and brother killed for breaking laws *because* they were sent away . . . not to mention you call them Worms. That's a bit insulting."

Carlos snorted. "The Worms have become their own people.

Dirty and violent and cruel. You cannot just . . . invite them back. They do not belong there."

"Well . . . it sounds like you did some bad stuff too. No offence."

Carlos glanced at him, scowling. "We are the King's People."

"Maybe you should tell your King to lighten up."

Eric instantly regretted his words. He tensed, wondering if Carlos would turn on him to defend his King's honor. The cave-dwelling boy was taller, more muscular, and carrying his knife and long, deadly sword again. Eric would have no chance if he attacked.

Instead, Carlos just laughed. "Yes," he said, "maybe I should." He turned ahead and kept walking. "But you must understand, these matters are from our fathers."

Eric shined his light over a patch of yellowish moss growing out of a deep crack. He wondered if they were getting near a forest again. They were definitely heading *downward*.

"I keep hearing a lot about your father and his father and so on. Who cares what they did?"

"They are our ancestors . . . ," Carlos said, looking at him in surprise.

"And my ancestors lived in caves and—" Eric stopped, horrified. "Sorry."

Carlos frowned. "Your ancestors lived in caves?"

"Sort of. *Our* ancestors, by the way. When you get down to it, you and I have the same ones. The point is, we don't have to listen to our dads."

Carlos stopped and met Eric's eyes. "You don't understand. It is the Law."

"And who made the Law?"

Carlos paused. "Juarez Santi. The first—"

"King," Eric finished. "Yeah. That's what I thought."

This time he had gone too far. Carlos stiffened and pointed a finger hard against his chest.

"You don't know the Midnight Realm," he said quietly.

Eric recoiled a little, flushing. "No . . . I don't. I just—"

"You don't know us," Carlos cut in. "You come from the surface. How could you?"

Eric didn't know what to say. He turned away from the boy's intense gaze, and Carlos dropped his finger and started down the tunnel again, his hand resting on his knife. Eric hurried to catch up, wincing as he did, and made a mental note not to talk about the King anymore. They walked in silence for a while, and then Carlos abruptly stopped.

They had come to a sharp ledge that dropped about twenty feet. It was pockmarked with cracks and crevices for handholds. Still, it was a long fall if they slipped.

Eric stared at the drop hesitantly. He wasn't a big fan of heights.

"We need to descend here," Carlos said, his tone still a bit chilly. "Can you make it?"

"Yeah," Eric said reluctantly. "Sure."

Carlos started down the ledge, gripping the cracks with his

hands and using his feet to carefully pick out the way below him. He moved easily, never slowing. Eric grimaced, put the cell phone in his teeth for light, and started down the ledge after him. *Sam would not be afraid.*

The ledge was steeper than it had looked at first, and Eric was careful to grab firm handholds as he went, since his left ankle was sore. He was moving very slowly.

Carlos reached the bottom and looked up.

"Come on," he called. "You're almost there."

"Easy for you to say," Eric muttered.

He grabbed onto a jutting rock, balancing his right foot and taking a cautious step down, always feeling with his toes. He hated climbing. Eric took another short step, finding a crevice for his right hand. He grabbed onto it and gingerly felt for another hold with his shoe. He had just settled on a half-decent spot when he felt something big moving on his hand.

Eric turned, pointing the cell phone in his teeth, and the light fell on a huge black scorpion sitting on his right hand, watching him. Its tail was curled up over its body, the venomous, glistening stinger poised to strike. Eric shouted and instinctively yanked his right hand away, flinging the scorpion, and he felt his left hand slip from its perilous handhold.

Then he was falling, and he felt the ground slam into his spine.

Fifteen Hours After

SILVIA STARED AT THE STRANGE, DARK-EYED GIRL, wondering where she had come from. The fur-clad men and women adjusted their crude weapons, looking uneasy. Brian just stood there, trembling and white-faced.

"Speak, demons," the girl snapped.

Her blade was dangerously close to Brian's throat. Silvia saw tears stream down his face, and the girl pulled him in, gripping the stone knife tightly.

"Let him go!" Silvia said, stepping forward. Her knees were shaking.

"Are you the leader, demon?" the girl asked sharply.

Silva took another tentative step forward. "I guess. And I go by Silvia, thank you."

The girl seemed to consider that. "Fine. Why have you come here?" She gestured to Brian again. "This one can barely speak, he quivers so much. He is a like a fish on the line."

Silvia watched as the other people behind her shifted again. They almost looked . . . afraid.

"Do you . . . live down here?" Silvia asked, meeting the girl's coal-black eyes.

"Of course, demon," she spat. "And you are from the surface. We know this."

"What is your name?"

"Lower your weapon," the girl said, pulling the knife tighter against Brian's throat.

Silvia realized she was talking about her flashlight. They were scared of the flashlights.

"It's not—" Jordan started behind her.

"Quiet," Silvia said sharply. "We'll lower our weapons, but we want our friend back."

She lowered her flashlight a little, and the girl eased the knife on Brian's throat.

"Now," Silvia said, taking another step forward, "what is your name?"

The girl stared at her, as if weighing her options. "My name is Jana. Why are you here?"

"Jana," Silvia said slowly. "Okay. We were touring the caverns with our teacher, and the floor gave out in the earthquake. We're just trying to get out again. If you can just let him go and show us—"

"You lie," Jana said. "If I let him go you will turn your weapons on us. You will destroy the Mother and bring death to us all."

Silvia exchanged a look with Tom beside her, frowning. "We don't even know you."

"But we know you," Jana snarled. "Have you seen anyone else down here?"

"Like who?"

"Men . . . women . . . a boy," she said. "Have you seen any of them?"

"No," Silvia said. "You're the first ones."

She saw the cave-dwelling men and women muttering among themselves behind Jana, their dark eyes fixated nervously on the flashlights. They seemed ready to run at the first hint of a threat. Jana glanced at her people, and then turned back to the class, pulling the black stone knife flush against Brian's throat again. He whimpered and lifted his chin away from the blade.

"They are a deadly people," Jana said softly. "They look like us, but they are beasts. They are armed. Do not let them get close to you. If you see them, turn your weapons on them immediately, or you will surely die."

Silvia heard the rest of the class whispering now, and their lights flicked around the dark.

"What about Brian?" Silvia said. "We want him back."

Jana hesitated, her eyes darting between Silvia and Brian like a cornered tiger.

She needs a little incentive, Silvia thought. She wracked her brain.

"How about a trade?" she said. "You know, in good faith."

Jana looked up at her. "A trade for what?"

Silvia tried to think. She couldn't give up a flashlight or they would figure out they weren't weapons. If they realized that, they might decide to attack and take them all prisoner. She needed something else . . . something they still might find interesting. The knife.

Silvia took off her bag and dug into her front pocket, pulling out the Swiss Army knife.

"This is a special tool," she said, opening it up. "A knife, scissors, screwdriver . . ."

Jana narrowed her eyes. "What would such a small knife do? I have better ones."

Silvia paused, taking a chance. "My father gave the knife to me. It means a lot to me."

That wasn't entirely true, since it was technically still *his* knife, but it was worth a try.

"It's a . . . family heirloom?" Jana asked slowly.

"Exactly. Yes."

Jana thought about that for a moment, and then nodded. "Bring it here."

Silvia walked forward, extending the knife with one hand. She held the flashlight in the other, ready to shine it at them and make a break for it. It wouldn't take long for these people to realize they were completely harmless. She reached Jana, eyeing the girl now that they were closer.

They were about the same height, though Jana was wiry and strong, with scars running along her arms and deeply calloused hands. She smelled faintly of dirt and damp vegetation.

"Let him go," Silvia said.

Jana released Brian, though she kept her own knife ready at his back. She stuck her hand out, and Silvia dropped the Swiss

Army knife into her palm. The two of them locked eyes as they did, measuring.

Jana tucked the knife away. "Remember what I said. Don't let them get close."

"Can you show us the way out?" Silvia asked hopefully.

Jana paused, exchanging another look with her people. She seemed anxious. Finally she pointed at one of the tunnels. "Go that way. It is a long walk, but stay as straight as possible. If you come across a village or see soldiers on the way, attack them immediately or you will die."

She abruptly turned and started for another opening, her people falling in quickly behind her. The last ones kept their crude spears pointed at the class, backing away to protect the rear.

"I wouldn't stay here long," Jana called, her voice echoing down the tunnels.

"Why?" Silvia asked.

There was no answer. Then Brian collapsed beside her, and the class rushed in to help.

They decided to ignore Jana's cryptic warning—they were cold, tired, and hungry. And if there really was a second group of dangerous humans down here, they needed to be ready for them.

The class had gathered together close to the shore, huddled in a small group for warmth. Many had shed outer layers to try and dry them out and Jordan was distributing a few morsels of food. Despite the run-in with Jana, they already looked more at ease now that they could stop and catch their breath. It was comforting to know what was hiding in the shadows . . . humans.

Silvia saw Derek refill his empty water bottle from the lake and chug it down again. A lot of the class was drinking freely from the lake now, but she was still waiting for another river.

"That girl was crazy," Ashley muttered, perched beside her on a rock. "That was so smart of you about the lights. I bet you they would have tried to eat us."

"I don't think so," Silvia said, "but it doesn't hurt for them to be afraid of us."

"I can't believe people live in this place!" Ashley said.

"I know. Mr. Baker would love it."

Ashley sighed. "Poor Mr. Baker. Well . . . at least we know the way out now."

"Maybe," Silvia said.

"You think she was lying?"

"I don't know. Just the way she said it. Why not lead us out herself?"

"They're afraid of those other people too. We have to watch out for them."

Silvia looked out over the water. "Yeah. I wonder where Eric is. . . ."

"Probably on a spit," Ashley muttered.

"Ashley!"

"Sorry," she said. "When did you start caring about that weirdo anyway?"

"He's not a weirdo. He's quiet."

"He's nuts."

Silvia scowled. "He tried to save my life. And a bunch of other people's too." She sounded a little more defensive than she intended and felt her cheeks burning. "He's part of the class, you know?" she said.

Ashley looked at her. "Yeah . . . sure. So what now, fearless leader?"

"I don't know. I think we should give people a little break. I am so tired."

"Me too."

They fell into silence for a bit, and Silvia allowed her mind to drift. She calculated how long they had been down there—it had been over fifteen hours. It felt like forever. She took out her water bottle and took a long drink. It was nearly empty.

She wondered what her parents were doing. She figured there was probably a rescue operation underway. Maybe a crowd had formed at the visitor center: journalists and families and curious onlookers. She could picture her worried mom waiting there.

Actually, she was probably in a tunnel somewhere up there with a pickaxe. Silvia smiled at that image and then thought back to early yesterday morning before she had left for the school trip.

"Sil!" her mom had shouted as she went to the door.

Silvia had sighed and looked back. "Yeah?"

She rushed over with a plastic bag. "Snacks, Silvia. You forgot them. I packed you two water bottles, a granola bar, and an apple, since you said you were getting lunch and dinner."

"Thanks," she muttered, feeling like a little kid again. She shoved them into her backpack.

"Are you excited?" her mom asked.

"For a bunch of caves?" Silvia said sarcastically. "Thrilled."

Her mom smiled and gave her a little push on the arm. "Be nice. I think it will be fun. Oh, your hair is already frizzing up." She immediately started adjusting it, trying to flatten it out.

"Mom," Silvia said, pulling away, "no more hair fixing."

"It's what mothers do. You should have worn that new shirt I got you."

"Mom, I'm not five anymore."

"I know. I just . . ."

"Thank you," she said sharply. "But I'm not. I'm okay. I know why you do it and . . ."

She trailed off. They had sort of an unspoken agreement not to talk about Silvia's issues. Her mom always wanted to, but the whole topic just made Silvia angry.

"I'm sorry," her mom said, the smile vanishing from her face.

Silvia felt guilty, but her dad was already waiting in the car. "It's fine. See you tonight."

And then she left in a rush, trying not to think about the fact that she had probably just upset her mom for the rest of the morning. And now Silvia might never see her again.

"How long are we staying here?" Mary asked, breaking the silence.

Silvia snapped back into the present. "I don't know. Maybe we should try to sleep for an hour?"

"Here?" Naj asked fearfully.

"Well, someone can keep watch," Silvia said. "I could use a nap."

There was a murmured assent around the group. Many were yawning and blinking.

"I'll keep watch," Ashley said. "There is no way I am sleeping down here."

"You sure?" Silvia asked.

She snorted. "Definitely. I am not sleeping for a second in this place."

"Good," Tom said loudly, "because I need a power nap."

He lay back on the ground, using his backpack as a pillow. A few others copied him.

Silvia patted Ashley's leg and lay out on the hard stone. It was uncomfortable, but she was so tired—physically and mentally—that it still felt very welcome.

"Wake me if you see anything," Silvia said.

"No problem," Ashley muttered, shining her light nervously on the tunnel openings.

"We'll be all right," Silvia said, closing her eyes.

"I hope so," Ashley murmured. "We have a track meet next weekend."

Silvia giggled. "You're ridiculous."

"I try."

"We'll be there," Silvia said. "And we're going to have a heck of a story."

Silvia tried to think of anything but the caves. She pictured herself running the track in front of a cheering crowd, the midday sun shining down on her skin, the air warm and fresh. The thought was soothing, and she felt herself drift into sleep. The track was still there, but then it grew darker, and she saw that the fans had all changed into huge black spiders.

They started crawling over the bleachers, and Silvia ran right into a great black web.

The image was shattered by a scream.

Silvia jolted awake, sat up, and looked around wildly. Her eyes widened.

Naj was sliding backward toward the lake, trying desperately to find a handhold on the smooth, rocky floor. Something enormous was pulling him into the lake.

Fifteen and a Half Hours After

CARLOS WATCHED HELPLESSLY AS ERIC SLAMMED into the ground. His backpack caught most of his upper body, which saved his head from hitting the rock. Eric groaned and rolled onto his side, his hand pressing against his lower back.

"Are you all right?" Carlos asked, kneeling beside him.

Eric managed a nod. "I think so. Just got the wind knocked out of me." He rolled onto his stomach, still holding his back tightly and grimacing. "Did you see the size of that scorpion?"

"Yes, a juvenile," Carlos said. "They're still tasty if cooked over a fire."

Eric looked at him in horror. "A juvenile? How big are the adults?

"Depends," Carlos said, helping him to his feet. "But smaller than the Black Deaths."

Eric winced as he straightened up again, and then shined his light on the cliff face. More bugs were crawling out of the cracks and crevices now: horned black beetles, disturbingly large centipedes, and a few more of the terrifying-looking scorpions. Eric almost gagged at the sight.

"You know, I am starting to wonder if it's as nice as I thought down here."

Carlos laughed. "There are not so many bugs near my village. Ready?"

"Just give me a minute," Eric said, slowly stretching. "I feel ninety years old all of a sudden." He readjusted his backpack and rolled his shoulders. "Wait . . . what's a Black Death?"

Carlos's smile slipped away. "Very, very large spiders. They have claimed many lives."

"Yeah, I think I'm going to go ahead and leave the caves," Eric muttered.

"There is still much beauty to see," Carlos replied. "Come on. We need to hurry."

The tunnel continued to dip here, and Carlos knew they were not far from the Forbidden Lake now, or the Room of Light. The other surface humans would likely find their way to one of those two large chambers . . . almost all the tunnels led through them at some point. But what about the Worms? Did they know about the surface humans? They shouldn't, as none were allowed in the Realm, but if they had heard something or caught a glimpse of light, Jana may have led them out.

"Are you okay with heights?" Carlos asked suddenly.

Eric paused. "Like . . . higher than what we just climbed down? Why do you ask?"

Carlos led them into a wide cavern, and Eric's light fell on its centerpiece—a massive, seemingly bottomless chasm.

"Whoa," Eric murmured.

Even Carlos had to admit that it was a daunting sight. The chasm was some fifty feet across and could only be traversed by a very narrow shelf that ran along the far wall. More than one Worm had been tossed into the pit for punishment in the last hundred years—Carlos had even attended one such execution as a boy. He still remembered the screams fading away.

"The Great Hole," Carlos said. "Not too creative a name, I suppose."

"Makes sense to me," Eric replied, his voice small and tinny in the huge chamber.

"We will cross there," Carlos said, pointing to the crooked ledge.

"You can't be serious," Eric said.

"It will take hours to go around and connect to the other side . . . precious time that we do not have. And we would have to climb back up that wall with the scorpions . . . your choice."

Eric eyed the chasm. "Let's go for the ledge," he said reluctantly.

"Good," Carlos said.

He led them to the ledge and stepped out confidently. The ledge itself varied from two feet to about a foot wide at its narrowest point, but Carlos had crossed it many times before. It was simply a matter of keeping your back flush against the wall and sidestepping your way over.

"Just follow me," he said.

"Oh boy," Eric murmured. "You sure about this?"

"Yes." Carlos started across, moving carefully for Eric's sake. "It's an easy walk."

Eric gulped. "Right."

Carlos made his way forward, stopping constantly to allow Eric to catch up. Eric was shuffling just a few inches at a time, his eyes locked on the endless abyss. He held his light in one trembling hand, lighting his way, and he was blinking feverishly as sweat poured down.

"You're doing fine," Carlos said.

"Yeah," he said weakly. "No problem."

And then his light died. Eric cried out in panic, and Carlos grabbed his arm.

"It's okay," he said, giving him a reassuring squeeze. "Just follow my lead."

"I can't see anything."

Carlos couldn't either. The glare of Eric's light was still sitting in his eyes. But he knew the way. Clutching Eric's arm, he continued forward, pulling a muttering Eric along with him.

"Almost there," Carlos said.

His soft voice echoed again and again until the encouragement was lost beneath them.

"I am really trusting you here," Eric managed, his voice quivering and hoarse.

"And do you?"

There was a long pause. "Yeah . . . I guess so."

Carlos reached his foot out and felt open ground, and he helped Eric step off the ledge.

"See," Carlos said. "That wasn't so bad."

"Never again," Eric muttered darkly. "What a perfect time for my cell phone to die."

"Don't worry . . . I will lead."

"I prefer to have light, thank you. Especially when there are giant bottomless pits!"

Carlos's eyes began to adjust again, and he saw Eric digging through his bag. "Could have really used that flashlight . . . a granola bar . . . water bottle . . . tuna . . . stupid tuna! Why would I bring a can of tuna, honestly? Now if it was . . . wait."

Carlos frowned. "What?"

"The tuna is in olive oil," Eric said delightedly. "I can make a light!"

"Should I know what tuna is?" Carlos asked.

"Probably not. Am I anywhere near the cliff?"

Carlos pulled him a few feet farther. "There."

Eric abruptly sat down, and the glare faded completely from Carlos's eyes. He knelt down, watching as Eric clumsily took out the can and punctured the top with a piece of stone.

"Is that flint?" Carlos asked, recognizing the black color.

"Yep," Eric replied. "I read about a guy who did this once. Now, if I know my mom . . ." He reached into his bag and laughed. "Yep, a napkin."

"I don't understand," Carlos said.

Eric began folding the paper.

"So . . . did you guys always speak English?" he asked.

"The King's tongue?" Carlos said. "My grandmother told me

once that the people spoke a different language when they came down. Juarez spoke the King's tongue as well though, and he taught them that language instead. He said it was better to forget everything above. My grandmother also said it gave him power against the surface demons . . . people."

"Which is why you call it the King's tongue," Eric said, nodding. "Makes sense."

Eric stuffed the rolled-up paper through the small hole in the can, pushing it right to the bottom. He then flipped the paper around and put the other side into the can, waiting patiently.

"The oil is soaking through the napkin," Eric said. "Now the fun part."

He grabbed the flint and started hitting it with a metal fork; sparks flared out, and both boys turned away from the sudden blast of light. Eric hit the flint again and again. Finally, a spark landed and flames sprouted on the napkin.

It began to burn like a candle, pushing the darkness back.

"Sweet!" Eric said.

Carlos laughed. "Very clever. Are you ready to go—"

"Almost," Eric replied, digging something out of his bag. "Just a quick update."

He opened his book of lined paper, revealing his map. Despite their rush, Carlos was interested in the process—no one had ever bothered to create a map of the Realm before, and he knew nothing of the "explored sections" that Eric had pointed out earlier. It was as if the world he had always known was growing around him.

"Here," Eric said, offering the pen. "Add to the map. You know it better than me!"

Carlos examined the pen, holding it awkwardly between index finger and thumb, and tested it on the paper. A black line appeared seamlessly beneath it, and he looked at the instrument in wonder. They had once had ink and quills, but the ink had long since been used up. His grandfather had been the last to write anything down, other than on stone with milky barbar root paste.

"Go on," Eric encouraged. "Put these sections on there."

Carlos shook his head. "We must start again from the beginning."

He began to draw an entirely new map. He copied Eric's labels, taking a strange delight in drawing out the letters. "What is this thing?"

Eric followed his pointing finger. "Oh . . . a cactus. Well sort of. Art isn't my thing."

"A cactus," Carlos said slowly, nodding. "There."

He kept working, picking up speed now as his eyes darted from his map to Eric's. A few times he asked Eric for pointers on spelling, trying to remember his grandmother's old lessons. Occasionally he passed the map to Eric, telling him what to write before accepting it back again.

"These are the large tunnels," he explained. "There are uncounted smaller ones."

"The Warrens look interesting," Eric said, watching carefully as Carlos worked. "Like a maze. What's past that?"

Carlos hesitated, wondering if he should tell him about Medianoche. He just wrote *Our Lands*.

Then he sat back and smiled. "For a general idea, it is good enough. Have a look."

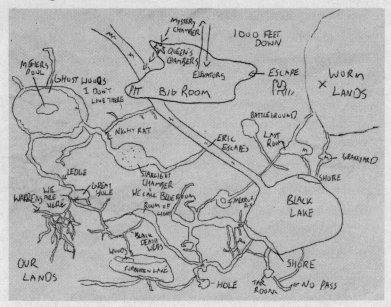

Eric read over the map. "Why are these Ms here . . . they seem kind of random?"

"Sometimes we also mark places where we find Worms trespassing . . . as a message."

Eric whistled. "There are still a lot of things to see."

"I told you," Carlos said proudly. "We will head for the Room of Light—"

He stopped, holding a finger up to his mouth to silence Eric as well. The sound was faint, no more than a whisper against the stone. But Carlos's ears were sharp. Someone was coming.

Carlos drew his sword from the sheath across his back, moving with practiced silence. He considered telling Eric to put out the light, but it didn't matter now. They had already been spotted. He rose to his haunches, gripping the bone sword with two hands, his eyes darting about.

Carlos heard it again: a brush against the stone from careful footsteps.

His eyes landed on a nearby opening. The Worm was approaching from there. He moved quickly toward it, cocking the sword, and stepped to the side, waiting to bring down his weapon for a killing blow. His stomach was heavy—he did not like to kill. But the Worms would not bear any such reservations. If they found the Midnight King, they would kill him instantly.

Another footstep. Carlos tensed, his fingers trembling on the hilt.

Then a tiny shadow stepped through the opening, and Carlos lowered his sword.

"Eva?"

Seventeen Hours After

FOR A SECOND, SILVIA THOUGHT SHE WAS STILL dreaming. But when Naj screamed again, she snapped out of the daze and leapt to her feet, feeling her heart pounding wildly through her chest. She had a distant thought that Jana hadn't been lying: They should have left the lake. Silvia ran through the stunned class and grabbed Naj's outstretched hand, trying to plant her feet and pull.

"Don't let go," Naj screamed.

Silvia got a better look at the attacker now. It looked like a nightmarish distortion of a catfish: long, curling whiskers prodding the ground, no visible eyes, and fins that were walking steadily toward the water like tank treads. It must have been ten feet long.

Silvia felt herself being pulled along with Naj.

In an instant Tom was there beside her, grabbing Naj's other hand and heaving backward. Naj screamed as the catfish tightened its grasp. Even with both of them, they were outmatched.

"It hurts!" Naj sobbed. The catfish's gaping mouth was wrapped around his kneecap.

"Help us!" Silvia shouted, looking back at the class.

Joanne and Greg ran over, grabbing onto Naj's elbows and trying to find steady footing. All of them were sliding along the stone, their shoes finding no traction. The catfish kept pulling.

"Hold this arm!" Silvia said to Joanne.

Joanne tightened her grip, and Silvia stepped forward and brought her shoe down on the catfish's fleshy gray head. The massive fish didn't even seem to notice. Its two pairs of squat dorsal fins just kept walking backward, pulling them all toward the water, where its huge forked tail splashed with anticipation, soaking them with more freezing water.

"Again!" Tom shouted.

They were almost at the water now. Silvia knew that if it pulled Naj into the water, he was as good as gone. They had to hurry. This time Silvia reached down, grabbed hold of the catfish's long whiskers, and pulled.

The catfish yanked its head away, releasing Naj's leg. It wrenched its whole body like it was caught on a line, and its huge head slammed into Silvia's waist. She went flying backward, slamming hard into the ground and feeling half her body splash into the icy water.

Silvia looked up, dazed, and saw the catfish coming toward her.

She rolled away from the water and tried to climb to her feet, but the catfish rammed into her torso. Silvia hit the ground hard again and attempted to crawl away. She heard grunts as Tom and the others ran to help, kicking at the enormous fish. Tom grabbed its slimy tail, but it flicked him off like he was nothing.

Silvia scrambled to her feet and climbed up onto an exposed rock, pulling herself up with every last bit of energy she had. The catfish took a last desperate bite at her legs, and then felt the sharp ledge with its long, prodding whiskers, realizing she had gotten away.

Slowly, almost reluctantly, the catfish slunk back into the black water and disappeared.

Silvia ran a soaking hand through her hair, shaking.

"Pack your stuff," she said. "We're getting out of here."

The group started off within minutes, leaving the underground lake behind. A few people had given Ashley dark looks or whispered comments for falling asleep on her watch, but Silvia had come to her rescue. Naj had a pronounced limp but was otherwise okay; catfish didn't have overly large teeth. A few small cuts and dark bruises on his leg were the only visible reminder of the attack, apart from his trembling hands and pale face.

As they walked out of the chamber, Naj turned to Silvia.

"Thanks, Sil," he murmured.

"Don't mention it," she said.

"You saved my life."

Silvia shrugged, embarrassed. "Anyone would have done it."

"But they didn't. You did."

Naj kept moving, helped a little by Jordan and Greg. Ashley shot her a supportive smile, and Silvia flushed. Everything had happened so quickly that she didn't even really have to think about it. How could someone so weak suddenly become brave? Or had she somehow changed?

Silvia dismissed the thought. The familiar bubble of fear was still sitting in her stomach, waiting to swallow her. She wasn't a hero. Her mind was fickle, and maybe that helped a little down here. But it didn't make her brave. And it was only a matter of time before her walls broke.

The group slowly climbed the tunnel, many of them locked in nervous conversation about the near miss by the lake. She saw that Tom, Derek, and Leonard were leaning down and staring at something on the wall. Silvia frowned and headed over, tailed by Ashley.

"What is it?" she asked.

Tom shrugged and pointed to the wall. There was another M drawn onto the rock there.

"What do you think they mean?" Derek asked, his eyes on the letter.

"I don't know," Silvia said. "But I bet Jana will know if we run into her again."

"You trust that scary girl?" Leonard mumbled. "She was about to kill Brian."

"She was right about the lake," Silvia pointed out.

Tom snorted. "She could have been a bit more specific. I don't trust her."

Silvia sighed. "No . . . neither do I." She noticed that the group was milling around ahead of them, waiting. "Let's get going.

We've got to stay together. If Jana was telling the truth and there are other people down here—"

She was cut off by a deep, booming rumble. Silvia recognized the sound immediately. It was the exact same noise they'd heard earlier in the Mystery Room—right before Mr. Baker had fallen. Silvia realized they had all forgotten something very important about earthquakes.

Aftershocks.

Seventeen and a Half Hours After

ERIC RELAXED AS A SMALL, WIRY GIRL STEPPED INTO the meager light of his tuna-torch, her face spotted with dirt and rivulets of sweat. Her long dark hair was knotted and thick and tied back into a loose ponytail. She wore hide pants like Carlos's, along with something like a black leather jerkin exposing scrawny arms. She also had a bow and arrow strapped around her shoulders.

Carlos looked stunned. "What are you doing here?"

"You didn't think I was going to let you run off alone, did you?" she asked scornfully. "I just didn't realize you were going to head in completely the wrong direction to start with. I've been looking for you where the demons were sighted, but you run off to the Ghost Woods—oh!"

Her dark eyes flicked to Eric, and she grinned, walking toward him.

"A surface human," she whispered. "You don't look like a demon."

"I don't feel like one either," Eric replied, climbing to his feet.

"This is Eric Johnson," Carlos said. "His class fell in the—"

"What is your shirt made of?" Eva said.

Eric looked at Carlos for support. "Umm . . . cotton, I guess."

"We don't have that," she mused. Her eyes fell on his running shoes. "What are those?"

"You need to go back to Medianoche," Carlos said. "The Worms could be . . ."

"They are already here," Eva said, turning back to him. "I saw them."

Carlos stiffened. "Where?"

"They were crossing through the Warrens. Ten of them, including Jana."

"*Haga,*" Carlos muttered, staring out over the yawning chasm. "Where were they headed?"

"Toward the lake," Eva said. "Obviously, one of them spotted the demons." She stopped herself and turned to Eric thoughtfully. "Sorry, old habit. I thought surface humans were old white men with beards."

Eric laughed. "Another myth, I'm afraid. Though we have those too. The ones down here are all students. We fell into your caves after the quake."

"Interesting," she said, feeling his sweatshirt between her fingers. "Oh . . . I like this."

Carlos scowled and pulled her back, turning her to face him. Eric saw fear in his eyes for the first time. "Eva . . . you need to get back to Medianoche. Tell the soldiers to be on guard—"

"Are you going to send me back through the Warrens alone?" she asked. "With the Worms walking around? If they find me, even *I* may not be able to hold them all off, Brother."

Carlos hesitated, and then swore again and started to pace. Eva flashed Eric a wink.

"No . . . it is too dangerous," Carlos said at last. "You will have to stay with us."

"I agree," Eva said. "For you two as well. You could use a real warrior for this mission."

"How old are you?" Eric asked incredulously.

She puffed up, meeting his eyes. "Nine years old, and I could beat you in a fight any day."

Eric laughed. "I don't doubt it for a second."

"This just keeps getting better," Carlos said. "We must get to the other surface humans quickly. Eva, stay close. Eric, you can keep the light, but prepare to put it out at my warning."

"Fair enough," Eric said.

Carlos turned to one of the jagged openings. "And keep an eye out for the Worms," he said solemnly, sheathing his sword and drawing a knife instead before stalking toward the tunnel.

"He's become very dramatic since he became King," Eva whispered to Eric.

"King?" Eric asked, watching as he slipped into the shadows.

"He didn't tell you?" Eva said. "Not surprising. Come on, Surface Boy!"

She scampered after Carlos, and Eric frowned. "Eric . . . my name is Eric."

* * *

"Beautiful," Eric whispered, looking around the chamber in awe.

It was covered in intricate white stone structures, some form-ing chandelier-like stalactites, others stalagmites like translucent coral, and where they met, pillars that gleamed like diamonds. The formations created reflections on the rocks as well—distorted and disorienting as a fun house. The small flame of his tuna-torch reflected around him, creating eerie floating lights.

"We call it the Room of Light," Eva said, following close behind him and watching his reaction. "Sometimes we come here with torches, and people just sit here and stare at the light."

She had stayed close to him the entire walk, quizzing him on the surface and his clothes and what weather was like and how did they stand so much light. She could talk endlessly.

Eric looked up at the shadowy formations on the ceiling. It had been an hour or so since he had lit the tuna can, and it was still burning. It even had a slightly fishy aroma, which had Eva desper-ate to try some. She stared at the can again now, eyeing the flame.

"Is it going out yet?" she asked.

"I don't want it to go out, remember?"

She shrugged. "I want to try it."

"Once it is out," Eric said firmly. "Carlos?"

"Over here!" he called, his soft voice echoing through the room. "Your friends were here."

Eva and Eric exchanged a look and hurried over to find him crouched on the ground, holding up a granola bar wrapper. He showed it to them, frowning, and looked down a tunnel.

"Oh, great . . . they're littering," Eric said.

Eva took the wrapper and licked it. "Hmm," she said. "Not as exciting as I thought."

Carlos stood up again, deep in thought. "If they went that way, they would come to the lake, as I suspected . . . but they would have to cross through an area full of Black Deaths. That would be bad for them. We'll follow them. If they're not there, we'll have to track back."

"And if we come across the Worms along the way?" Eric asked. "Your *Majesty?*"

Carlos stiffened, and then turned to Eva. "You told him."

"I thought it might be important for him to know," she said, crossing her arms.

"Why didn't you mention that before?" Eric asked.

"I don't know," Carlos said dismissively. "It didn't seem important."

"Important?" Eva said. "If the Worms see you they won't stop until they kill you."

"Perfect," Eric muttered.

Carlos hesitated, and then turned away, shaking his head. "It didn't matter. *Doesn't* matter."

"Why?" Eric said.

"Because he doesn't think he's a good King," Eva answered.

Carlos glared at her. "It's not that simple, Eva. . . ."

"Actually, it is," she replied.

"This was my fault," he said sharply. "I showed mercy."

"Mercy?" Eric said, frowning.

"Never mind," Carlos said. "Now let's get moving again—"

He was cut off by a deep rumble beneath their feet. The noise soon spread, until it was emanating from the walls and ceiling as if they had been swallowed whole.

Eric immediately understood. "Aftershocks," he shouted. "Get out of the chamber!"

But the shaking intensified before they could move. Eric heard something shatter and caught a glimpse of one of the great pillars tumbling to the ground. Cracking and splintering noises filled the cave. Despite his own warning, Eric felt like his feet were planted in the stone, and he could only watch as the formations fell around him. He heard another awful *crack*.

Looking up, he saw that one of the massive formations had broken off directly above his head. It wrenched free and dropped, and Eric knew that he was about to die.

But Eva was fast.

She slammed into him like a linebacker, knocking them both out of the way as the formation hit the ground and shattered. Eva half-led, half-dragged him into one of the tunnels, where Carlos was already waiting. Soon, the shaking faded again, and Eva stood up, dusted off her pants, and shot Eric a lopsided grin.

"Looks like you owe me one, Surface Boy."

Eric wiped his face, hardly believing how close he had just come to death. His body shook.

"Eric," he managed. "And thank you."

Beside him, Carlos was staring at the broken chamber, his face ashen.

"What have I done?" he murmured. "I have undone all my forebearers' work."

"You?" Eric said, looking at him incredulously. "What are you talking about?"

Carlos was silent for a minute, unwilling to even meet Eric's eyes. Finally, he spoke in a halting whisper. "I spared a Worm," he said. "I am sorry. The Mother has punished us since."

Eric frowned. "With earthquakes?"

"Yes," Carlos said. "I have brought this on us all."

Eric climbed back to his feet, shaking his head. "You didn't cause these, Carlos. King or not. These are called earthquakes. It's just the tectonic plates shifting. They happen all over the world. We don't get many in New Mexico, but in California they get a ton. That was just an aftershock. I should have expected them. It probably won't be the last one either, now that I think about it. They're obviously pretty severe this far down into the Earth, which makes a lot of sense, really." He smiled and patted Carlos's shoulder. "Trust me: This wasn't about you, man."

Carlos stared at him, his mouth moving silently. "But my father always said—"

"Listen," Eric said, "your father might have been a great guy and a good King . . . I'm sure he was. But you're not him. Me, I don't want to be anything like mine. We shouldn't be spending our whole lives trying to be exactly like our parents. That won't work."

"Surface Boy is right," Eva said. "You need to stop quoting Father ten times a day."

Carlos looked between them, obviously reluctant, and then turned back to the shattered Room of Light. Broken gemstones littered the floor like a sparkling carpet. "I am the King."

"Yeah," Eva said. "King Carlos Santi. And we need him right now."

"King Carlos Santi . . . ," Carlos repeated numbly. He nodded. "Yes."

"Exactly. Now stop moping, and let's go save Surface Boy's friends," Eva said.

Eric sighed. "Eric."

Carlos laughed and grabbed Eric's shoulder. "I'm glad you came, Eric Johnson."

He straightened and turned to go. Then a shadow fell across his face again, and he knelt down and picked something up. Eric leaned in for a closer look. It looked like a large half-eaten beetle.

"What is that?" Eric asked warily as Carlos rolled the beetle between his fingers.

"Haga beetle," Carlos said. "A very . . . unpleasant creature. Perhaps the worst of all. If one beetle gets a taste of blood it begins to hum, attracting the rest of the horde. They swarm over everything in a ravenous bloodlust. The biggest horde of all lives in a chamber in my Realm, but most of the other hordes live in the Worm lands. They are very common there."

Eva abruptly pulled out her bow, fitting an arrow and aiming it down the shadowy tunnel.

"What does that mean?" Eric asked, confused.

"The Worms eat them, especially when they are on the move. The Worms were here, heading down this very tunnel. And there is only one reason they would head this far into the Realm." Carlos stood up. "They have found your friends."

Eighteen Hours After

THE WALL OF RUBBLE SETTLED, CREATING A misshapen barricade. It had split the class in two.

Silvia looked around. It was only her, Ashley, the twins, Leonard, Derek, and Tom on this side. Jordan, Naj, Brian, Shannon, Greg, and Joanne were on the other.

She rushed forward to the wall of rock, looking for openings or loose stones. She found a small crack that seemed to lead through, but when she attempted to move the boulders around it, they didn't budge. The shattered pieces were large and heavy, even for an entire group to try to move. They would need an excavator to get through the rock mound.

She glimpsed Jordan on the other side through the crack. "Are you okay?" she called.

He nodded. "A couple of people have cuts and bruises. You guys?"

She glanced back at Leonard, who was clutching his leg. It

looked bad, and she felt her stomach turn when she saw blood on his shaking fingers. "Broken leg, I think," she said quietly.

Jordan scanned the wall of rocks. "I don't know if we can move this."

"We might as well try. Guys, come here."

The twins reluctantly came over, followed by Ashley and Derek. Tom was still consoling Leonard. They tried to clear a path, but only managed to move a few of the smaller outlying rocks. The big boulders felt like they were sealed with mortar. Silvia strained until her back hurt.

"Anything?" she called.

"No," Jordan called back. "It won't budge."

Marta wiped her sopping forehead. "We'll have to find another way."

"We said we wouldn't split up," Mary said.

"Too late for that," Silvia replied grimly.

Silvia went back to the crack and peered through, catching a glimpse of Jordan looking at his map. "Just wait there for us. We'll see if we can find another tunnel and meet up with you."

Jordan nodded. "Fine."

"We need some of the food," Mary said, looking through the opening.

Silvia saw Jordan's expression change. "How much food?"

"Well, we get more," Marta said. "We have seven people and you have six."

Jordan looked back at the group on his side of the wall. "Yeah . . ."

Silvia could see where this was going. She felt her stomach grumbling.

"Jordan, give us some of the food," she said coolly.

He looked at her, paused, and then dug in his bag and passed two granola bars through.

"Here," Jordan said. "You'll be fine. We'll be out soon."

"This isn't even close to half," Silvia said, scowling. "And we're the ones walking."

Jordan shrugged. "We don't have much left. I'm sorry."

"Jordan—" Tom said from where he was helping Leonard.

"That's all we can spare," he said, not meeting Silvia's eyes. "You'll get back here soon."

"You're a real hero," Mary snarled.

Jordan ignored her. "Get comfortable, everyone. They'll be fine."

Silvia just shook her head. She heard a brief discussion through the crack, and then the other group started laying out their stuff and plopping onto the ground. Silvia turned to her group. Between them, they had only three flashlights—hers, which Joanne had given her, Mary's, and Tom's. The batteries in all three had to be getting low. She was already using Ashley's batteries.

"How is he?" she asked, going to Leonard's side.

"Ankle's broken," Tom said. "I think I can help him walk. We don't have a choice."

"I'll take the other arm," Derek said.

"This is not good for my athletic career," Leonard added weakly.

Derek rolled his eyes. "What career? You're the fifth leading scorer."

"I was trending upward," Leonard snarled.

Together they slipped under each of Leonard's arms and hoisted him up, trying to move as slowly as possible. Leonard cried out in pain as they lifted him, and Silvia almost gagged when she saw the bloodied wound on his ankle. The falling boulder had struck hard and deep.

"Lead on," Tom said, nodding at Silvia.

"Does anyone have a marker?" Silvia asked.

They dug into their bags, and Marta found a Sharpie. Silvia tested it on the rock and drew a large X.

"You burying treasure?" Derek asked sarcastically.

Silvia gave him a look. "I'm going to mark the way . . . just so we know how to get back to them if we can't find another way around. Everyone ready?"

"Can't wait," Leonard managed.

Silvia reluctantly started back the way they had come. They had passed a few openings, nothing more than low, jagged holes, but they had decided to stick to the tunnel, as it seemed to lead upward. Now they had no choice but to try one of the other passages, and they all went *down*.

They walked until they found the first opening, and Silvia tentatively led them through, watching for webs and bats. She marked the wall every time they turned. They were moving slowly, and she could hear Leonard struggling. His constant gasps and yelps of pain turned her stomach. He needed rest.

They started down the new passage, which was marked with sparkling white flecks like snow. There was no moss or lichen here, which she took to be a good sign. Every time the tunnels turned green, a man-eating creature or forest was not far away. Finally, they emerged into a small chamber—the stone a pale orange and littered with bumpy, damp stalactites. Silvia thought they looked a lot like snot. But a little stream bubbled along one side, nestled into the stone floor.

"Let's take a little break," she said. No one argued.

As they were walking in, she noticed another crooked M carved into the wall.

"I hope these mean it's safe in here," she said.

Leonard cringed as Derek and Tom tentatively set him down against a stalagmite. They sat down beside him, along with the twins and Ashley. Silvia took a last look around the chamber and then sat next to Ashley, placing her nearly empty backpack behind her. She sighed.

"I'm tired," she said, rolling her ankle to try to loosen the tight muscles.

"Me too," Ashley replied.

Tom was checking Leonard's ankle.

"Just a little cut, really," Tom said.

Derek snorted. "What are you, blind? It's, like, a five-inch gash. He must have lost—"

"Dude!" Tom said. "Not helping."

"You guys have great bedside manner," Leonard grumbled.

Ashley turned to Silvia. "Think we can really find the others again?"

Silvia sighed. "I hope so. We can follow the Xs. The problem is that just gets us back to the wrong side of the rockfall."

"I hate caves," Mary said.

Silvia smiled and leaned back against a stalagmite, looking up at the orange ceiling, which was partially illuminated by one of the twins' wandering flashlights. "This part is nice."

"Debatable," Mary muttered. "I hope I never see a cave again after this."

"Me too," Ashley agreed.

"My dad thought this was going to be fun," Silvia said.

The day before the trip he had called her over to the computer to show her pictures of Carlsbad Caverns. He had gone there when he was a kid and had always been fascinated by it.

"Are you going to be . . . all right down there?" her mom asked from the kitchen.

Her dad frowned. "She'll be fine. What do you mean?"

"You know what I mean."

Silvia glanced at her, annoyed. "I'm right here."

"Honey, what if you have . . . an episode?"

"They can happen anywhere, Mom."

Her mother nodded, forcing a smile. "But if it's down there, it could be worse."

"Stop scaring her," her dad said gruffly. "She's fine."

Her dad always thought she was perfectly fine. He said so

all the time, and he was thrilled when the doctor seemed to confirm it. Why did her mom always have to remind him?

Silvia felt her temperature rising. "What am I supposed to do? Sit at home?"

"I was just saying . . . ," her mom said.

"That I'm a nut who can't even go on a field trip," Silvia finished. "I know."

Her mom sighed. "You know that's not the case. You just have to be aware."

"Trust me, I'm aware. Thanks for making sure."

With that she had stormed upstairs, ignoring her mom's apologies. She'd slammed her door and plunked down her on bed, hating that her mother reminded her of the episodes every time she went somewhere, and hating more that she was right. Why did she have to be crazy? Why did she have to have panic attacks? And was she really going to let them run her life?

So she had decided to go and prove them wrong. And now here she was.

I really showed them, she thought miserably.

She considered that for a moment. Maybe she had.

"So did my dad," Tom said. He put on a deep dad's voice. *"Son, those caves are a natural wonder. Rare chance to check them out, Tommy. Take some pictures now. Have fun."*

Silvia laughed. "Is that what your dad sounds like?"

"Pretty much," Tom said. "My mom is more like, *Please be careful. Tie your shoes. Don't go near any crevices; I don't want to have to come looking for you. Watch out for bats!"*

Silvia laughed. "That's a pretty good mom voice."

"Better than my mom," Marta said. She turned shrill. "*Don't you try and go exploring! You and your sister are always getting into mischief. I do not want to get a call from the bowels of the Earth saying that they have lost my daughters. I might just leave you there.*"

Mary giggled and then shook her head. "So much for that." She seemed to get a bit somber, and looked up at the ceiling. "I wonder what they're doing up there. Our parents, I mean. Are they all up there talking and waiting and stuff?"

Silvia sighed. "I have no idea," she said. "But I would love to find out."

Eighteen Hours After

"WE ARE DOING EVERYTHING WE CAN," OFFICER Brown said for what felt like the hundredth time. "But the caves are still unstable. We cannot begin rescue efforts yet."

He hated having cameras in his face, and he resisted the urge to scratch his cheek. It was itching terribly, probably with sweat. He imagined he looked about as awful as he felt. Eighteen hours now since the quake, and he'd slept for about three of them. The parking lot was a circus. Reporters, families, onlookers, a whole portable city had been set up. Trailers and vans dotted the desert like cacti, and more vehicles were pouring in. He was quickly losing control of the area.

"So, you have mounted zero rescue operations," a reporter asked, raising an eyebrow.

Thanks for making me look useless, Officer Brown thought. *Why don't you go down there and have a peek?*

"No," he said instead. "As I mentioned, we don't have clearance to go in there yet."

"So, what are you doing?" another reporter asked, one of the ten in front of him.

He hesitated. "Waiting. And praying. Thank you."

He probably wasn't supposed to end things so abruptly, but he didn't feel like answering any more questions. He'd never been great with reporters.

Officer Brown headed for the portable police trailer that had been set up by the natural entrance to the caves. At least it had a coffeemaker and some chairs. But he didn't make it inside. Three people stormed over to him, two men and a woman.

He recognized them immediately. Parents. *Here we go.*

"Don't you think it's time we go down there?" the woman said.

He tried to place her. *Ah . . . Mrs. Pike. Tom's mother.*

"We are still waiting on the geologists to—"

Mr. Pike flushed red. "You've been saying that for a day now. We'll go ourselves!"

"The area is off-limits," Officer Brown said tiredly. "Listen, I understand—"

The other man, Mr. Rodrigues, pointed a finger at the officer's chest. "No, you don't. My daughter is down there in those caves. She . . . she has medical issues. Anxiety. It's time we go down there."

Officer Brown didn't blame them. He'd be saying the same thing. But the orders from the chief had been very clear: No one goes into the caverns until the geologists clear the area. Period.

And now he had to try and keep these families calm. He had spoken to all of them already: the Tams, the Lewskis, the Robinsons. Even the Bakers—the teacher's parents. The worst of all was Ms. Johnson. She just sat in her car, her forehead bandaged, and stared blankly at the cave opening. He had made the decision to move the headquarters to the cave's natural opening—it was deemed a safer eventual entry point than the elevator shafts, which had been damaged in the quake. By the same token, they assumed any survivors would come out that way. But all they ever saw were bats, great black clouds of them that swept into the sky like a tornado.

"I'm sorry," he said. "I am. But we should know very soon."

"You'd better," Mr. Rodrigues said. "My wife and I are not going to wait much longer." He turned as if to gesture to his wife, and then frowned. "Where did she go now?"

"Brown!" someone called.

Officer Brown turned to see an officer waving for him. Behind her, he caught a flash of black hair as somebody sprinted into the caves.

"Oh no," he muttered, and took off after her.

"Told you!" Mr. Rodrigues called. "Honey, I'm coming with you!"

Mr. Rodrigues and the Pikes started after them, and Officer Brown waved to the other officer. "Hildi, stop them, will you. Mrs. Rodrigues! That area is off-limits!"

As Officer Hildi blocked the stampeding families, Officer

Brown ducked under the police lines and ran into the cave—a huge, arching entrance cut into the stone landscape. He could hear shouting and caught light flashes in the corners of his vision. The reporters had already caught on. *Perfect.*

"Mrs. Rodrigues! Get back here!"

She ignored him, running deeper and deeper into the caves. She was a hundred feet in when Officer Brown finally caught up to her, grabbing her shoulders and pulling her to a stop. She shrieked.

"Get off me! I am going to find my daughter!"

"I can't let you do that."

She turned to him, scowling. "Just try and stop me!"

"I'm coming, honey!" Mr. Rodrigues shouted, racing into the cave.

"Hello?"

The voice seemed to come from far away. It was almost ghostly.

"Did you hear that?" Mrs. Rodrigues whispered, looking at him.

"Stay here," Officer Brown said firmly. This time Mrs. Rodrigues listened.

Feeling nervous sweat beading on his forehead, Officer Brown hurried deeper into the caverns. The passageway sloped downward here, and it was strewn with boulders and debris.

"Who's there?" he called.

He knew he shouldn't be going into the caves, but there was no choice now.

"Over here," the voice called again, weak and faint.

Officer Brown raced toward the sound, running through a narrow tunnel. If there was another aftershock now, he knew he could be trapped. But he kept moving.

"Here," the voice said again, growing faint.

Finally Officer Brown spotted a shadow sprawled on the floor. He raced over and found a man lying there, one of his legs twisted behind him. He had been crawling.

Officer Brown turned him over, and the man gave him a weak smile. He recognized his face immediately from the photos.

"Mr. Baker?"

The man gave him a tired nod. When he spoke, his voice was a hoarse whisper. "The class . . . are they here?"

Before Officer Brown could speak, Mr. Baker's eyes closed, and his body went limp.

Nineteen Hours After

CARLOS EYED A BLACK STRAND OF WEB AS HE stepped carefully around it, every muscle tensed.

"Be careful," he whispered.

They were picking their way through the lair of the Black Deaths, and he bore his sword in one hand and his knife in the other. Eric's light was dim now—just enough to illuminate the tar-black strands that lay within some of the tunnel openings. Eva was moving slowly at the rear, her bow drawn and taut with an arrow.

Despite his best efforts, Eric could not match their stealth. His breathing was loud and ragged, and his shoes scuffed against the stone. Carlos just hoped the noise wouldn't stir anything in the darkness here. He preferred to avoid this area altogether and ordered his people to do the same. There was nothing worth finding in this part of the Realm.

Carlos stopped when he heard a muttered "ugh" and a *twang*.

He whirled around and saw Eric yanking his foot away from a strand. He was stuck.

Eva realized it too. "Oh, Surface Boy."

"We need to go," Carlos said urgently.

He stepped forward and brought his sword through the strand, slicing it cleanly in two and freeing Eric. But they weren't fast enough.

A shadow moved in the corner of his eye, and Carlos turned just in time to see a Black Death rushing toward Eric, ready to claim its prize. He reacted without thinking.

Carlos slashed with his sword, slowing the creature, and Eric cried out in fear as his light fell on the monster with its gnashing, foot-long fangs. Eva pushed him into a run. Carlos drove the Black Death back, jabbing again and again, his eyes darting around at the same time, looking for more. Eric found one first.

He was wrenched sideways by an outstretched, hooked leg that gripped his shoulder and pulled. He stumbled to the ground, and the giant spider emerged from another mass of web, descending on him with greedy eyes. But before its fangs reached him, an arrow thudded into the side of the spider's head. It hissed and thrashed and then went still, and Eric scrambled up.

They took off running again, and Carlos gave a last swipe with his sword and followed.

"That's two, Surface Boy!" he heard Eva shout.

The three of them sprinted toward the Forbidden Lake. When they were far enough away, Carlos called for them to halt, seeing Eric struggle. They were at a crossroads: A smaller opening led back toward the Warrens and the Great Hole. The entrance was squat and uneven, however, and Carlos suspected the surface humans would have taken the main tunnel toward the lake. They would follow them there.

As soon as they stopped running, Eric doubled over, grabbing his sides and wheezing.

"Thanks, Eva."

She patted him on the back reassuringly. "Any time. You should try running more."

"Yeah," he managed.

Eva leaned against the smaller opening, adjusting the yew fletching on an arrow.

Carlos just smiled and shook his head. "That was close. It was lucky you didn't—"

"We can't stay lucky forever," a voice said.

Ten Worms emerged from the opening, including Jana, who put a knife to Eva's throat. Carlos stiffened with fear at the sight. The other five spread out, spears pointed at them. Carlos noticed they seemed leery of Eric and were staring at the small flame from his tuna can.

"Drop it, Eva," Jana said sharply, her eyes locked on Carlos. "Now!"

Eva hesitated, and then let her arrow fall to the ground.

"Let her go," Carlos warned, his fingers shifting on his weapons, itching to attack.

"So, you have found the demons," she said, glancing at Eric. "As have I."

"What did you do to them?" Eric demanded, stepping forward.

Three spears pointed at his chest, and he stopped, taking a step back again.

"I sent them on their way to Medianoche," she said innocently. "They wanted some directions, so I provided them. Of course, your people will fear the surface humans, won't they, Carlos? Captain Salez may lead an attack on them. There may even be a battle. With their strange weapons, many of your people will die. With some luck, maybe all of them."

Carlos looked beyond her, thinking of Medianoche. She was right: If they stumbled on the town, Captain Salez would attack. Carlos had left him that exact order. But she was wrong about their weapons. Eric's people were defenseless. It would be a slaughter.

"What are you doing in my Realm?" Carlos asked quietly.

Could he possibly get to Jana before she struck? Could he kill so many Worms?

"My nephew spotted them on his way home," she said. "You know him, Nennez."

"The boy in the woods," Carlos murmured, his knees almost buckling.

"Yes, whom you spared for trying to feed himself. I suspect it was simply for sport. Let my nephew go and then allow your hunters a chance to train. Well, your trick backfired, boy. Nennez spotted the surface humans on his way back and hurried to tell me. I do love an unexpected opportunity."

Carlos tightened his grip, enraged. His mercy had led to this.

His weakness. And now his sister was in danger. His father had been right: A Midnight King had to be *strong*.

"The quake split the surface humans, and we split as well to track both groups. Thankfully, I heard your shouting. Stupid to be so loud, Carlos."

She brought the knife closer to Eva, whose lip was quivering in anger.

"And here we are, with a mighty gift."

"You already sent the surface humans to Medianoche," Carlos spat. "You'll get your war, though you don't understand what you have done. You don't need her."

"Insurance," Jana said coolly. "If the battle doesn't come, we will just negotiate instead. I want new lands, Carlos. I want access to the Ghost Woods and to the Black Lake. Understand? Don't follow me. If you do, she will die as soon as you come near. I promise you, Boy King."

She began to back away, and her Worm soldiers followed, their spears jutting out.

"Take me instead," Carlos said. "What better tool for negotiation than the King?"

"No!" Eva shouted.

Jana frowned. "You? Who will negotiate with me then?"

"Captain Salez. He would have to free me."

"Take both," one of the Worms snarled, a thick, squat man with a beard past his chest.

"Then there is no deal," Carlos said, turning on him. "And you will die first."

Jana seemed to consider. "Fine. Drop your weapons."

Carlos handed his sword and knife to Eric, who accepted them with trembling fingers.

"Carlos . . . ," Eric said.

"Stay with Eva," he replied, meeting Eric's eyes and willing him to find his friends before they could get to Medianoche. "Do not follow us. Wait by the Forbidden Lake for me to come."

He squeezed Eric's arm and turned back to Jana. "Let her go."

One of the Worms stepped forward, putting a knife to Carlos's throat, and then Jana pushed Eva forward, almost causing her to stumble. Eva scooped up her arrow and turned, preparing to lunge at Jana.

"Don't even think about it," Jana warned, adding her knife to Carlos's chest. "Let's go."

As one, the Worms backed down the tunnel, and Carlos locked eyes with his little sister until the light faded and she vanished into darkness.

"The boy is too dangerous awake," Jana said. "Knock him out."

Before Carlos could move, he felt something hard connect with the back of his head.

Nineteen and a Half Hours After

ERIC WATCHED CARLOS DISAPPEAR INTO THE SHADOWS, and then spared a look at his tuna-torch. The flame was nearly extinguished now—just a tiny, flickering orange tongue. He shook his head.

"I'm sorry, Eva. . . ."

She turned to him, her eyes flashing. "About what? Let's get moving."

Eric was confused. "To go wait by the lake?"

"Don't be a barbar root. We're going to go find your friends. There are other ways than crossing the lake. Leave your light. Where we're going, you're going to need both hands."

"But your brother said to wait. . . ."

"He was being sneaky," she said in exasperation. "Do you even understand what's happening right now?"

Eric gestured vainly down the tunnel. "They took your

brother. And Jana sent my friends to your village. But they don't have any weapons . . . they're just lights. There won't be a war. . . ."

"No, there won't," Eva said grimly. "Just a massacre."

"What are you talking about?"

"When my brother left, he told Captain Salez that if the surface humans came to Medianoche, that meant something had happened—that the surface demons had overpowered him or killed him and were coming for us. He told him to defend the city . . . to kill the intruders."

Eric felt his stomach tighten. "But . . . they'll see that they are just kids. . . ."

Eva shook her head. "My people have been raised to fear you. They have heard stories of your weapons. My brother and I are . . . more open-minded than most."

"Why?"

She hesitated. "My mother . . . she was different. She didn't believe all the stories, or at least, she said that people change. I think she wanted to go back."

"To the surface?"

"Yes. But she died five years ago. Some illness. Some people said it was punishment."

"I'm sorry," Eric said.

"The point is, Captain Salez has orders. He won't even let your people get close to the village. They will slaughter them with arrows and spears before they have a chance to speak."

"No," Eric whispered. "We have to go!"

She threw her hands up. "What did I just say, Surface Boy? Come on!"

With that, she took off in the other direction, leaving Carlos and the Worms behind her. Eric reluctantly blew out his torch, shoved the now-burned-out tuna can in his bag, and took off after her. The darkness was complete once again, and he had to move carefully, using his hands to guide him. His ankle was still sore, but the brace was holding fast and he was able to jog.

"I can't see, Eva," he called.

"Ugh!" she replied. "It's like bringing my baby cousin on a rescue."

Suddenly he felt a small hand in his, and she led him on. Soon after, Eric walked right into her, her bow jamming into his chest painfully.

"Thanks for the heads up," he muttered.

"You still can't see?" she asked incredulously.

"There is literally zero light down here."

"Your eyes can adjust," she replied.

"Yeah, maybe in nine years," he said. "I've had a day."

She snorted, grabbed his hand again, turning him to the right. "Now we duck . . . low."

Eric did as he was told, and they started down another tunnel. His head was bent over almost to his waist, and he felt rocks brushing against his back and shoulders. He started to feel claustrophobic, and squeezed Eva's hand a little harder, anxious to get out of the enclosed space.

"Are you trying to break my fingers, Surface Boy?"

"Where are we?"

"This tunnel runs beside the Forbidden Lake and meets up with a tunnel on the other side. I think that's where Jana sent your friends. From there they could head right to the village."

"How much farther?" Eric asked reluctantly.

Eva seemed to think about that, as if running calculations. "An hour."

"Great," he muttered. He knew that an hour bent over like this would feel like months.

"You must be excited to see your friends," she said, clearly trying to change the topic.

Eric paused. He didn't really want to get into that . . . but they had time. Unfortunately.

"Yeah . . . well . . . they're not really my friends."

"What?"

"I mean, we're in a class together. We're just not really friends, technically."

"None of them?" she asked. "You don't even have one friend?"

"No," he said, flushing. "To be honest, they probably don't care that I'm missing."

"That's not true," Eva said.

"No, it is. I'd be surprised if they even noticed I was gone."

Eva was silent for a moment. "Why? You seem nice, Surface Boy."

"Eric," he corrected, sighing. "I don't know. I guess . . . it's kind of my fault."

"Duck lower," she said, and Eric quickly did as he was told. "Why is that?" she asked.

"I like being alone."

Eva laughed. "My grandma told me that only lonely people say that."

"I'm not lonely," Eric said, "I just think it's . . . safer that way."

"Because of your father."

Eric started. "How do you—?"

"Because I listen, " she said. "Your father left you. Now you think fathers stink, and because of that, everybody stinks. So you figure you should avoid everybody."

"Are you sure you're nine?"

"Carlos says that too," she said. "And Grandma says I have the mind of an old lady." She squeezed his hand. "The problem is if you avoid everybody, how are you supposed to know if they're any good or not? My mother and father died. But I won't ignore people because they might die. Then I would be very lonely. You can't avoid people because you think they might hurt you. You'll never know unless you take the chance to find out."

"Yeah," Eric said. "But keeping my distance . . . it's just . . . easy."

"Stupid things usually are," she said simply. "I bet your people are looking for you."

"They're not."

"We'll see," she said. "Even I like you, and my father told me you were a demon."

Eric laughed. They continued through the narrow tunnels, turning and dipping and crawling through new openings like scurrying rats. The walk seemed endless, and Eric felt his back aching and his thighs burning from the strain of staying so low. Finally, when he was beginning to wonder if he could continue at all, Eva held a firm hand to his chest, stopping him.

"Stand up, Surface Boy."

Eric did so gingerly, and then sighed aloud when he could straighten and even stretch his hands over his head. His whole body seemed to expand with a deep ache. "Where are we?"

"Back in the main tunnel," she said. "It's a straight shot from here. Just one small chamber on the way with orange rock. We should hurry. Are you ready to jog a little?"

"Not really."

"Well do it anyway."

She grabbed his hand again and took off, and he had no choice but to follow.

"Do you have many friends, by chance?" Eric asked sarcastically, wheezing.

"Not really," she said. "But I have a real reason."

"And what's that?"

She laughed. "No one can keep up with me!"

She picked up her pace, and Eric did the same, shaking his head as he ran. They ran until his sides were burning, until Eva whispered in a hushed, urgent voice: "There!"

Eric looked up and saw light—a white, brilliant glow on the rocks.

Flashlights.

Twenty-One Hours After

SILVIA RELUCTANTLY CLIMBED TO HER FEET, watching as her flashlight flickered and struggled to stay on. She knew it would die at any moment. They had been alternating for a while now, but it had simply been too long. Mary's and Tom's lights would be close behind, and then it would go dark.

They would be blind, and if they ran into Jana again, she would know that they didn't have weapons after all.

"Time to start moving," she said, turning to the others.

She helped Ashley up and watched as Derek and Tom propped Leonard up between them. He had mercifully gotten some sleep, and even Silvia had felt her eyes growing heavy. It had been almost a full day since the earthquake, and everyone was exhausted. But the last time they'd slept, someone had almost died. She wasn't about to make that mistake again.

"Which way?" Marta asked.

There were two openings set into the orange chamber, and

Silvia eyed them warily. Jana had simply told them to head straight down the passage, but she had neglected to mention the fork in the pathway. Silvia walked past both openings, shining her meager light into the dark.

"I don't know," she admitted.

"Jana said straight," Ashley said. "I think it would be that one."

She pointed to the larger of the tunnels, which was rounded and smoother. Silvia stared into the shadows, wondering why there was an uncomfortable tingle running down her neck. She felt . . . uneasy. But Ashley was right. On closer inspection, the other tunnel veered off to the right twenty yards down, disappearing around an upward, sloping bend. Jana must have meant the other one—but both options felt wrong.

For a moment, Silvia felt the weight of everything pressing down on her. Mr. Baker and Eric disappearing, the near-drowning in the river, the creatures and Jana and the aftershocks. She thought of the endless rock above her head, always waiting, and the stale, cold air choking her.

The bubble of fear moved into her throat and her eyes fogged with tears.

"I don't know," Silvia murmured. "I don't know what to do."

She turned back to the others. Tom and Derek had Leonard walking again, though they all looked exhausted. Everyone did: pale and clammy with dark circles under their eyes.

Leonard looked faint and stumbled as they moved him forward.

"I'm sorry," Silvia said. "I tried . . . we should have just stayed where we were. . . ."

She felt the first tears spill down her face, and she turned away, wanting to run, wanting to crawl into a hole and hide. She hunched over, holding her throat and her chest because everything felt tight. The air seemed thin now. She crouched, mouthing a silent plea for help that she was too embarrassed to voice. The panic had finally overtaken her.

To her surprise, it was Tom who crouched down beside her, his hand on her knee.

"It's okay," he said quietly. "You've done everything you could, Sil."

"I can't breathe," she said.

"Panic attack," Tom replied. "It will pass."

She looked at him, confused. "How . . . ?"

"My dad," he said simply. "He gets them sometimes. Listen . . . you kept us going down here. You saved Brian and Naj's life. You are the bravest person I've ever seen."

"I'm not brave," Silvia said, wiping her face. "Look at me. I get these constantly. I get them at home when I'm watching TV, in the bathroom, in bed. I'm always afraid. *Always*."

It was the first time she had ever told anyone except her parents and her doctor. As soon as she said it, she wanted to take it back. She didn't want to be crazy. She didn't want them to pity her or be afraid of her. She felt new tears welling . . . now she had ruined the one place she felt normal.

But Tom didn't pull away or give her a pitying look. He just smiled.

"Well, then you're even braver than I thought."

Silvia thought about what he said, and began to take deep, full breaths. At first, they were unsteady and difficult, but they soon began to flow more easily, and the panic started to fade. Tom stayed beside her, but he didn't stare or look afraid. He just waited. Finally, she nodded.

Tom smiled and extended a hand. "You ready?"

She took his hand and let him pull her up. She wiped her eyes again, straightened her clothes, and turned back to the others. Ashley was watching, clearly bewildered, but she gave Silvia a hug and squeezed her hand, smiling.

"Good," she murmured, "you're human after all. You were starting to freak me out."

Silvia laughed, and with that, the fear was gone. "Yes, I'm human."

"You can talk to me, you know," Ashley said quietly.

"I know," Silvia said. And for once, she meant it. She turned back to the tunnels and made her choice. "We'll keep going straight," she said, leading them on. "Stay close."

The group plunged into the wider tunnel, and as they walked, Silvia caught a whiff of something filtering down the passage. She breathed it in and picked up her pace, baffled. She knew the smell: smoke. It smelled like the wafting, pungent scent of a campfire.

"Do you smell . . . ," Marta said.

"Fire," she said excitedly. "There's something up there! Come on!"

The group picked up their pace, even Leonard, and Silvia felt her spirits rising. The smell was growing stronger now . . . she thought she could even smell something like charred, roasting meat. Her mouth watered. Was it Jana and her people? Or someone else . . . Eric or Mr. Baker?

"Turn out your lights!" a whispered voice commanded. "Do it now!"

Silvia whirled around, panicked, and everyone else did the same. When their dim, struggling remaining flashlights fell on two figures behind them, her eyes widened.

"Eric?"

Twenty-One Hours After

CARLOS OPENED HIS EYES AND INSTANTLY FELT his head pounding. It was like a swarm of bats was spiraling around his brain and screeching madly in unison. His body shook with the slow, plodding steps of someone carrying him, and the headache grew worse.

He struggled to remember what had happened. The Worms. The hit on the head. He tried to feel the back of his head, but his hands were bound. He looked around and saw two men walking on either end of him, one holding his arms and the other his legs.

"He's awake," one man grumbled.

"That's fine," Jana said from the lead. "Boy, if you speak we will put you out again."

"There will be . . . punishment for this," Carlos managed, squinting as his head throbbed.

"No, I think not," she said. "Either the surface demons will destroy your people, or we will negotiate for your release. I told you what I want: real lands to feed my people."

"And you think we will honor that once you turn me over?" Carlos said, furious that they had knocked him out.

"Likely not," she said, turning back to him. "We will exchange you for other hostages."

"You won't get my sister. . . ."

She laughed. "Yes, yes we know. But your grandmother perhaps. And you have cousins." Jana turned ahead again. "But let us hope that won't matter. Hopefully, the surface demons will burn Medianoche to the ground and there will be no need to negotiate at all."

Carlos fell silent and tried to will the pain to pass. The strain on his arms and legs was terrible. The two Worms were far from careful and kept letting his tailbone smack painfully against the ground. A few of them were speaking, and he tried to listen, but the pain in his head was too distracting. Instead the words came through in segments:

". . . think they're almost there . . ."

". . . what about the sister . . ."

". . . those weapons would be handy . . ."

". . . the hogtied King . . ."

". . . I say we kill him now . . ."

Finally, the group slowed to a halt. Carlos looked past them and saw that they had arrived at a small chamber they called the Hollows, not far from Medianoche. Voices echoed here, spilling into the tunnels in all directions. Jana looked around, as if trying to get her bearings.

"We will keep him here for a bit," she said softly. "If he shouts, knock him out again."

The men set Carlos down and he rolled onto his side, trying to take some pressure off his sore tailbone. His head was still throbbing with pain, and he cursed himself for being so stupid. He should have left his sentries on the borders. This many Worms would never have been able to cross unseen. He had been too worried about the surface humans and not his own people. His father would be furious.

To make matters worse, Jana was marching the surface humans to their deaths. Despite everything, he had doomed them as well. Even if Eric was right and his mercy had not brought about the quake, it had still condemned the Realm to disaster and death. He was right all along. He was too weak to be the King.

Jana crouched down in front of him. "What did the other boy tell you?"

Carlos met her eyes stonily. "That his people did not come here for a fight."

"Why did you not kill him? Were you afraid?" Jana asked.

"He broke no Law, unlike you, Worm."

"Your father would have protected your people. He would never have allowed this."

"You didn't know my father," Carlos said quietly.

"No," she said. "But I know that Midnight Kings have cursed my people for a century."

"That is your fault," Carlos said, meeting her cold black eyes. "They were exiled for breaking the Law, in case you forgot."

She took his chin with her sharp nails, digging them into his skin. "That is the fault of your arrogant ancestors. They sent us away because we did not honor the rule of a false king. Because we thought we came down here for freedom. But instead they called us *Worms*. Outcast to the worst lands, where we feed on undergrown Night Rats and bitter haga beetles."

"Traitors deserve no better," Carlos said. "My father always said so."

"The tide has turned."

She turned as Nennez jogged into the tunnel, wheezing. He too bore a knife.

"Gapa said you would be down here," Nennez said, his eyes falling warily on Carlos.

"And here we are," she replied, turning back to Carlos. "Watch him, Nephew. Porcho, Fania, come with me. We're going to see if the surface humans are getting close."

With that, she hurried down an adjoining tunnel, the two Worms close behind her. Nennez stepped forward, and Carlos hoped for some mercy. Instead the boy quickly put his knife to Carlos's chest like he was a wild rat for the spit. He was as bloodthirsty and savage as the rest.

Carlos had learned yet another lesson: Mercy did not have a just reward.

I am sorry, Father. I have failed you, he thought for the hundredth time since the quake.

His thoughts turned to Eva and Eric. Would they actually go to the lake and wait?

No. It was Eva. She would try to save Eric's people and rescue Carlos. And despite his terrible fears, he knew that Eva was resourceful, and that Eric was also very clever. They still had a chance.

He had no choice but to wait. It was up to them now.

Twenty-One and a Half Hours After

"COME ON," ERIC WHISPERED, WAVING THEM BACK. He was looking beyond the class for any movement. Eva had already warned him that the group was dangerously close to Medianoche.

"What—" Silvia started.

"Silence," Eva cut in, motioning down the tunnel. "Follow me."

Eva led the group down the tunnel, walking until they were back in a small chamber with orange walls. As soon as they were through, Eric turned to the class and was immediately engulfed in a hug. With a mixture of shock and delight, he realized it was Silvia.

"We thought you were . . . well . . . and you tried to grab us . . . ," she said.

Then she pulled back, her cheeks turning pink.

"I'm glad you're okay. We looked for you, but we were so lost."

Eva snorted, and Eric gave her a dirty look. "I . . . well, I'm okay," he stammered. "Where are the others?"

"We got split up," Silvia said. "What happened? Why did you take us back here? And who is this girl? Is she with Jana?"

"Don't say that name," Eva spat, fuming. "I am Eva Santi. My older brother is the Midnight King. He was with Eric for a while. Jana is a Worm, and you were all about to die."

Silvia looked between her and Eric. "The what King? Die? What do you mean?"

Eric quickly explained what Jana had intended, and how Carlos's soldiers would have killed them all. At the news, Ashley paled and sat down on the ground, shaking her head.

"I knew she was bad news," Tom said quietly.

Eva walked up to Silvia, eyeing her. "Are you the leader here, Surface Girl?"

"Silvia," she said, hesitating. "Yes, I guess so."

"Fine. Now Jana is going to send a scout to see if you made it to Medianoche. When she learns that you haven't, she will send someone to my village to tell them they have the King and want to negotiate for his life. When that happens, it's going to get ugly around here." She gestured toward Medianoche. "The soldiers are going to head out and they won't be happy."

"So what do we do?" Eric asked.

"Take this group up this tunnel," she said, pointing to the smaller opening. "You will come to a chamber called the Catacombs. Don't go in there . . . just wait nearby. I think Jana will bring Carlos there."

Eric frowned. "Why?"

"It has meaning for her. More importantly, it has built-in

protection against attack. If she arrives before I get there, tell her you took a wrong turn. Say nothing about your weapons . . . just stall her there."

"Where are you going?" he asked.

"I am going to find Captain Salez," she said. "We'll come back for Carlos."

"Okay," Silvia said. "But why don't we just stay here and wait for you? It's safer."

Eva hesitated. "If the soldiers see you, they might attack. They are afraid, and they will be enraged that Carlos was taken. I can't call them off. The only person who can is my brother."

"Be careful," Eric said.

Eva smiled and grabbed his arm. "You too, Surface Boy. This one is pretty and seems to like you," she said, nodding at Silvia. "I told you. You're very nice for a demon. See you soon."

She took off running down the tunnel, and Eric quickly turned away to hide his burning cheeks from Silvia, who was looking at him with a bemused expression.

"Making new friends?" she asked.

"Something like that," Eric said. "Come on . . . let's get to the chamber. The others . . ."

"Should be safe," she said. "They're on the other side of a rockfall."

"Good enough."

Eric started up the tunnel, and the rest of the group followed, all of them looking beaten down. Silvia stepped up beside him, using her flickering light to guide the way.

"It sounds like you've been busy," she said.

"Well, I found a chamber of glowworms, a giant rat, a forest, I fell off a cliff because of a scorpion, crossed over a bottomless pit, was almost eaten by a spider, and oh, I met a King."

Silvia laughed. "I think it might have been the same spider that almost ate me. We saw a glowing whale, Naj was almost eaten by a catfish, we found a forest too, and met cave people."

"So pretty close," Eric said.

"Pretty close," Silvia agreed. "Oh, and we found a bunch of Ms written on the walls everywhere. You see any of those? I've been trying to guess what they stand for."

"They stand for the Midnight King. It meant you were in his Realm."

Silvia snorted. "It's been quite the field trip. Mr. Baker . . . ?"

"No . . . unfortunately not." Eric watched as her flashlight played over the walls. "It wasn't all bad, I guess. There was some pretty cool stuff in the mix, besides all the almost-dying I did."

"Agreed," she said. "I even found a few other things. I didn't expect as well. About me, I guess. It seems that everything I thought about myself got . . . well . . . turned around down here. Like maybe I was a bit hard on myself. And some of the secrets I was hiding . . . they don't seem like such a big deal anymore. Do you know what I mean?"

Eric turned to her. "Actually, I know exactly what you mean. And now I'm ready to go home."

"Yeah. I . . . look!"

Her light washed out over a chamber ahead, and they slowed

to look. The chamber was about the size of a football field, and the ground was pockmarked with cracks and holes. Silvia stepped out, but Eric grabbed her arm and pulled her back. Something about the place felt weird.

"Eva said don't go in, remember? She's usually right."

"So what do we do now?" Silvia said, taking a step back.

Eric looked out over the chamber. "We wait."

Twenty-Three Hours After

JANA STORMED BACK INTO THE CHAMBER, HER black eyes narrowed to slits. She had her knife drawn and was clutching it at her side, as if ready to strike.

"The demons did not go to Medianoche," she hissed.

"I guess they're too smart for you," Carlos said, smiling.

He pulled away as she leaned into him. "They were heading there. One of my scouts saw them. Your meddling little sister must have warned them." She stood up straight again and cut the vines on his ankles. "Stand up. We're moving."

"Where?" he asked, slowly climbing to his feet.

His hands were still tightly bound and chafing against the vines, so he struggled to keep his balance. Jana met his eyes—she was the same height.

"For my insurance," she said. "We are heading to the Catacombs to negotiate."

"The Catacombs," Carlos said slowly. "Where your father—"

"Was executed by yours," she spat. "Yes. And where the haga beetles should prevent any foolish rescue attempts from your soldiers. One drop of blood, and no more King."

Carlos grimaced. "That's a dangerous game, Jana. We could all die."

"The Mother will protect us," she snarled, "her *righteous* children."

"You can still release me," Carlos said. "I will let you return home."

"Home is a wasteland," Jana said. "There is no food, little water. Only the fear of the demons has kept us from leaving the Mother. We cannot live there. We want access to the rest of the Realm. We have as much a right to it as you do. Worm or not."

"Traitors have no rights."

"There you go with that word again," she said. "Who had Nennez betrayed? He was born in the Worm lands. So was Fedo over there. And what about the others? Your father exiled Nina because she refused to acknowledge her brother's crimes. My father was killed because he did not bow. My brother for hunting in the Ghost Woods. Are they really *traitors*?"

She leaned in, her breath hot upon his face.

"I do not acknowledge the Midnight King. You do not rule me. Only the Mother does."

She turned and started for another tunnel opening, gesturing to her people.

"Bring him. If he tries anything, make sure he only does it once."

As they stepped out into the Catacombs, Carlos looked down warily. None came here if they could help it. The haga beetles had carved the floor into a massive hive, tunneling deeper and deeper through solid stone with their powerful mandibles. There they lay dormant unless stirred.

"Keep walking," one of the Worms said, though he sounded nervous.

Nennez was pale beside him, carefully stepping around the many crevices and holes. On the far end, Carlos saw a white glow in one the tunnels and realized the surface humans were here. He looked for Jana and saw her crouching, her hand on the ground.

"Father, keep watch for us today," she said softly. "Help me change our fate."

Carlos watched her, frowning, and when she saw him she quickly looked away, as if embarrassed. But when she turned back, her eyes were hard again, and she led the group to the center of the Catacombs. There she stopped and gestured for Carlos to sit. He hesitated, until he felt a knife press against the small of his back. Then he reluctantly sat down, his eyes darting about.

"Weapons up and ready," Jana said. "Nennez, watch the King."

Nennez stepped in front of him, pointing a knife at Carlos's chest. Carlos looked up at him, and for a second he could almost see his father, standing behind Nennez imperiously.

This is what your mercy has bought you, his father seemed to say.

Carlos closed his eyes, ashamed.

"Demons!" Jana said, her voice carrying even at a whisper. "Come out!"

The lights in the tunnel suddenly flashed out into the chamber, and many of the Worms cursed and turned away. Carlos heard muttered conversations, and then two figures emerged.

It was Eric, along with a girl with long black hair. Eric had mentioned her: *Silvia.*

Silvia spoke first. "I guess you weren't trying to help us after all."

Jana paused. "I was simply pointing you at my enemy."

"Yeah, I gathered that," Silvia said coolly.

"Let the King go," Eric said, holding a white light but pointing it at the ground.

The Worms shifted nervously, and Jana turned to him, obviously uneasy. "This isn't your business, demon. This is a war that has been going on long before you got here. Just walk away."

"Carlos is my friend," Eric said.

"Don't be fools," Jana snarled. "One of my men has gone to get the King's soldiers to negotiate. Get out of here before they arrive. They will kill you all. That part was no lie."

"I will tell them to stand down," Carlos said, nodding at Eric. "They are friends."

Silvia raised her flashlight in warning. "Let him go, or I will be forced to use this—"

Everything happened fast. Her light suddenly sputtered and died, and Jana stepped forward and slapped the light out of her hand. Before Eric could move, Jana grabbed his arm and twisted until he let his flashlight fall to the ground. She put a knife to his throat.

"I told you to stay out of this," she whispered.

There was a stir in the tunnel, and Jana spun Eric toward the opening.

"Stay where you are," she ordered loudly, "or he dies. You can all wait there if you wish, but if you are smart, you will run away from here as fast as your legs will carry you." She turned back to Carlos, scowling. "When Captain Salez and your soldiers arrive, you will command them to drop their weapons immediately. If you don't, these two will die, and you will follow."

Carlos met her eyes. "Fine."

Jana looked around the chamber. "Now, everyone just stay quiet until—"

"Ow!"

Carlos turned to see one of the Worms kick his bare foot out, wincing. In the glare of the flashlight that was lying between them, Carlos saw a large beetle fly off. And then something worse.

A rivulet of blood running down the man's foot.

Jana seemed to realize it at the same time. "No," she murmured. "You fool."

A deep, resonating hum began to emanate from beneath them, growing louder and louder.

Jana let go of Eric and backed away, paling. "It's over," she said. "Nennez, kill him!"

"No!" Eric shouted.

Carlos started as Nennez turned to him, slowly lifting his knife for the kill. He met Carlos's eyes, but his bottom lip was quivering. Nennez just stood there, the knife hovering.

And so it all comes around, Carlos thought numbly. *I am sorry, Father.*

But Nennez didn't drive the knife into Carlos's chest. Instead, he nodded.

"A life for a life," he said quietly.

And then he cut Carlos's bonds. Carlos watched as the vines fell to the ground, and he turned his hands over, astounded. When he looked up at Nennez again, he didn't see hatred in the young boy's eyes as before, but he did see fear.

"Coward!" Jana shouted. "He's a murderer!" She started toward him. "Do I have to—"

The humming grew louder still, and the first beetles began to emerge from the deep.

Twenty-Three and a Half Hours After

SILVIA STEPPED BACK AS THE GROUND CAME
alive. It began to roil and move and quiver with activity as thousands of monstrous clacking beetles emerged like crude oil, spilling out across the chamber. She could feel the noise vibrating her bones.

For a long moment, it seemed that she and Eric could only watch with morbid fascination. And then the King shouted, "Run!"

His voice cut through the chamber, echoing over the terrible humming, and Silvia snapped into action. She tugged on Eric's arm and turned to the tunnel, where the others were shouting for them to hurry. The Worms broke for the tunnel as well, streaming past her wildly and kicking beetles off their exposed bare feet.

Silvia glanced back and saw Carlos scoop up the boy who had spared him, who had spilled onto the ground and was screaming. Carlos brushed off the beetles, slung him over his shoulder, and started running. All lines of battle were forgotten now—the group ran as one.

Silvia felt the beetles crunching beneath her feet and then cried out as one bit into her leg. She batted it off and kept running, trying desperately to keep her balance on the pockmarked floor. Jana ran beside her, terror written on her face. But she was only there for a second. Her foot slipped into a crevice and she spilled forward.

Silvia didn't even think. She turned back and knocked the swarming beetles off a shrieking Jana's face, grabbing her arms and heaving her up with every bit of strength she had.

The two of them ran together, bursting into the tunnel where the others were waiting.

"Go!" Silvia screamed.

They turned to run, Tom and Derek hoisting Leonard between them, and the whole mass of surface- and cave-dwellers ran down the tunnel, flinging off the last beetles. The humming was fading behind them now, but nobody seemed willing to stop. Silvia soon found herself at the front of the group, and as she rounded a corner she slid to a halt.

Eva stood there with her bow raised, flanked by at least twenty soldiers with bows, spears, and swords. A man stood at the front, his face scarred and weathered. He raised his right hand and pointed, his mouth opening with what was surely an order to kill them all, even as Eva raced forward to wave the soldiers off.

"Now—" the scarred man said.

"Stop!" a loud voice cut through, and the King pushed past Silvia, waving frantically. "Stand down. Jana, tell your people to drop their weapons."

The King's soldiers lowered their bows, but only partly.

Silvia saw Jana look around, surveying her options, and then nod. "Do it," she said.

Their weapons clattered to the stone, and Carlos led Silvia and the rest of the class forward, leaving the Worms to gather together in a protective circle. Silvia noticed the soldiers back away from the class fearfully before reforming to face the Worms.

"Your Majesty," the scarred man said, "the surface demons—"

"Are *not* demons, as I told you, Captain Stupid," Eva cut in, fuming. "You almost killed them!"

Carlos laid a hand on her shoulder. "They helped me, Captain. They are friends." He turned to the Worms. "We were nearly all killed by the Worms, however."

The soldiers raised their bows and spears again, and the Worms quailed together, looking ragged and pitiable. Except for Jana, who stood at the front, meeting the soldiers' eyes coldly. Despite her bites, she looked proud.

"The sentence is death," Captain Salez said, his eyes hard. "On your order."

Silvia watched in horror as their bow strings tightened. It would be a massacre.

Eric suddenly grabbed Carlos's arm. "Hey," he said. "You are not your father."

Carlos hesitated for a moment, and then he nodded. "No. I am not. Stand down," he said, gesturing for the soldiers to lower their weapons.

The scarred man turned to him. "But . . . the Law says—"

"I am the King," Carlos said somberly. "Stand down."

The men lowered their weapons, and Carlos walked toward Jana.

"What is this?" Jana snarled. "You want to torture us first? I will not bow to you—"

"There will be no torture," Carlos said. "Just an apology."

Jana looked completely taken aback. "A . . . a what? I won't apologize for—"

Carlos stopped before her. "Not from you. From me. I spent my whole life trying to be like my father. It was all I ever wanted. I pictured him in everything that I did. But Nennez just gave me a precious gift. I am not my father. I am Carlos Santi, the fourth Midnight King. And I am sorry."

The Worms looked at each other, muttering. Jana just stared at him. "What?"

"I am sorry. I am sorry that your families were sent away. I am sorry that so many of your people were executed. I am sorry that we have exiled you to starve. I am even sorry that we call you *Worms*. You are our brothers and sisters."

Silvia saw his soldiers looking bewildered. But Jana was even more confused.

"But we have fought. I just tried— "

"To kill me. I remember," he said wryly. "But when my

forefathers exiled your people, we made our own enemies. By the same token, I wish to make my own friends." He smiled. "I grant you access to the Black Lake and Ghost Woods. To anywhere you want to hunt. I invite you back into the Realm if you choose it, but I understand if you want to continue to live among yourselves. We will help you if we can."

Carlos raised his voice.

"I forbid calling them Worms from this day forth. Let them go. All of them."

Jana stood there for a moment, as if expecting a trick. When none came, she started pushing her people away from the soldiers. As they slowly moved back up the corridor, Jana turned to Carlos. Some of the anger had slipped from her face.

It made her look like a normal teenager again.

"You're right," she murmured. "You are not your father, Carlos Santi. You are a better King." She turned to Silvia. "And you, Silvia. Thank you. No demon would have saved my life. We were wrong, and maybe . . . maybe we have been wrong about many other things as well."

With that, she led the group away, and Eva rushed to her brother, embracing him.

"I'm proud of you, big brother," she said. "You became a real King today."

Silvia slumped in relief, and Eric leaned against the wall, wiping his face.

"Are you okay?" he asked, glancing at her.

"Yeah," Silvia said. "I think I am."

Carlos put his sister down and turned to the class. He was no longer smiling.

"You will all accompany me back to Medianoche. We have to talk."

Twenty-Five Hours After

THE CLASS SAT CLOSE TOGETHER IN WHAT Carlos had called the Great Hall, lit by the flickering light of a great fire in the middle of the room. The missing students—Jordan, Greg, Naj, Brian, Shannon, and Joanne—had been found by the King's soldiers and led back to the Great Hall, and though Eric noticed a little tension between Silvia's group and Jordan's, it faded almost instantly with the relief that everyone was alive. The soldiers had also searched for Mr. Baker, but had found no trace of him.

Almost everyone was sitting or lying around the fire now, full and content for the first time in almost two days. But Eric was still nervous. Despite his order to come talk, Carlos had left soldiers at the doorway and disappeared without a word. Eric wondered what was wrong.

He was deeply exhausted. Bowls of root vegetables and charred, stringy meat had been brought to them by Eva and her grand-mother, and they had devoured the food hungrily. Eric tried not to think about the fact that he was probably eating Night Rat, though it was so delicious that he wasn't really sure he cared.

Silvia was leaning against the wall, the firelight playing on her face. Like the rest of them, she was covered in dirt and sweat. Her hair was as knotted and tangled as the vines in the woods. She had barely spoken since they were led here an hour ago.

"Well, I think we have probably descended another five hundred yards," Derek said.

"Are you basing that on slope versus time or just a random guess?" Tom asked dryly.

Leonard, whose ankle had been freshly wrapped with some sort of yellow leaves, yawned and stretched. "A complete and total guess. I am thinking more like a thousand yards . . . at least."

"You're a meathead," Derek said.

"You're a goalie; what do you know?" Leonard replied.

"Hey, what did I say about that?"

Eric chuckled and climbed to his feet, plopping down beside Silvia. Somehow their banter was comforting. It had been a while since he'd heard anything so . . . normal.

But they made an important point: Carlos had never been to the explored sections, and the only way back was up the river. Could they even get back there? And more importantly, was Carlos going to allow them to leave? He had looked strangely somber on the way to Medianoche.

"Enjoy your rat?" he asked, glancing over at her.

"I prefer to think they have a herd of cows that I didn't see on the way in."

Eric laughed. "Yeah, good call. It does feel good to sit down for a while."

"It feels amazing," she agreed. "But I want to go home. What are we doing here? Do you think he's going to let us go? How do we even get out?"

"That's a lot of questions," Eric said.

She smiled. "Sorry."

"He's a good guy," Eric said. "I think he will. But . . . he might be worried."

"About what?"

"About his secret, about the people down here. I don't think that he wants to be found."

Silvia glanced at him. "That sounds ominous."

"I know. But we have the whole class together. That's a start."

"It is," she said, laughing. "And look at you over here, Mr. Talkative."

"Yeah," Eric said. "Somebody told me I should probably stop shutting everyone out."

"That sounds like a good idea," she agreed.

"What are you going to do when you get out?" Eric asked. "You know . . . first thing."

Silvia paused. "I think I am going to talk to my dad. I don't want to keep secrets anymore, you know?"

"What do you mean?" Eric asked.

She fidgeted with her hands. "Oh. Nothing. Just in general." She sighed. "No, I said I wasn't going to do that anymore. I have some . . . mental things. Anxiety and panic. It's . . . bad."

Silvia turned away, as if expecting him to laugh or move away. Eric frowned.

"That's okay. I had some problems when my dad left. So did my mom."

"Really?"

"Yeah. She went to therapy and took some medications. It's pretty common."

Silvia laughed. "You know, I haven't even told Ashley that. I was too embarrassed."

"I guess you just needed to get lost in a cave for a few days."

"I guess so," she said. "So how about you—"

She stopped as Carlos strode into the room, joined on either side by Eva and his grandmother. Carlos stopped at the doorway, surveying the students with a somber expression. Eric felt a little flutter in his stomach. Carlos's grandmother surveyed the food and smiled broadly.

"I told you they would like my cooking," she said.

Eva sighed. "I just said they wouldn't be used to it—"

"I have been cooking for sixty years. I know what children like to eat."

"I thought you always said they were demons," Eva said.

"Shush now!" her grandmother snapped.

Carlos exchanged a bemused look with Eric. To his surprise, Eric realized he thought of Carlos as a genuine friend—the first one he'd had since his dad left. And it was kind of nice.

"I am sorry for the delay," Carlos said. "But we have a problem that I had to consider."

The class straightened.

"I have been taught for a long time not to trust others or to show mercy. But of late, I am starting to see things a little differently." He smiled at Eric. "And so I will trust you, *if* you will agree to keep my people a secret."

There was a murmur around the room. Carlos held up his hands.

"I know you will want to tell people. I know it would be a great discovery. Eric has told me this. But this has been a lot for my people. We are happy here, especially now that the war has ended. This is our home, and we do not want to share it. If you tell others, they will come. Our world will change. We do not wish this." His dark eyes hardened. "I need you all to promise that you will keep our secret. It is *ours* alone to share."

"We will," Eric said. "I promise."

Carlos smiled. "I need to hear it from everyone."

One by one, they went around the room, and everyone promised to keep it a secret.

When they were finished, Eric stood up. "One thing," he said. "If he's okay, can we tell Mr. Baker? He will keep the secret, I promise you that. But trust me, he would love to know."

Carlos paused. "Okay. As long as you agree to make sure everyone keeps their word."

"Done."

"Is that the one you said was cute?" Carlos's grandma asked, nudging Eva.

"Grandma!" Eva hissed, flushing red.

Carlos sighed. "Now, I suspect you would like to go home."

There was a chorus of agreement, and the entire class jumped to their feet.

"How do we get out?" Eric asked. "Can we get back up at that river?"

Carlos shook his head. "No, I am afraid not. The way you came is impassable."

The class slumped. Ashley looked like she was about to cry.

But Carlos just smiled. "I borrowed something from you, Eric."

"What?" Eric replied, frowning.

Carlos brought his hand from behind his back. He was holding Eric's notebook.

"How did you get that?" Eric said, looking at his bag.

"We are very stealthy in the Midnight Realm," he replied. "Here."

Eric stepped forward, and when he saw the gleam in Carlos's

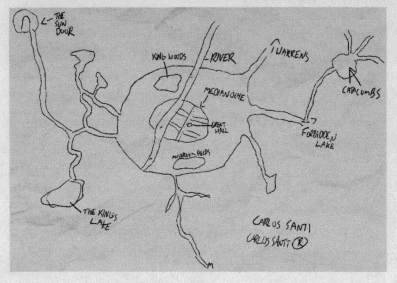

eyes, he opened it up and laughed. "You even signed it."

"Of course," Carlos said, giving him back his pen.

Eric read it and frowned. "Carlos, what is the Sun Door?"

Carlos and Eva exchanged a smile. "The way we came in. And now, one hundred and eighteen years later, we will open it to let you all out."

With a great heave, the soldiers rolled the boulder a mere two feet to the right, letting brilliant sunlight spill into the caves. They shouted and backed away from the line of sunlight that split the chamber in two. The class immediately stepped into it, bathing in the warmth. Carlos and Eva watched with wide, disbelieving eyes, and Eric laughed as Eva tentatively stepped forward to touch the light.

"It doesn't burn," she said in wonder. "It actually feels kind of nice."

"Carlos?" Eric said, gesturing for him to try.

Carlos shook his head. "Just the sight is enough for me. Maybe one day."

Silvia hugged Carlos and Eva, and then smiled at Eric and left him to say his goodbyes as the class began climbing through the narrow doorway into the waiting desert.

"You know which way to walk?" Carlos asked.

Eric nodded. "I think so. The visitor center should be east of here. The sun will show us."

"Good," Carlos said. He hesitated, and then stepped forward and hugged him. "I will always remember the day I saw a white light approach me from across the water. I have changed much since then. The entire Realm has. If you ever decide to come visit, you are welcome any time. But I cannot promise we will leave you alone. We could always use a bright mind in Medianoche."

Eric smiled. "I wouldn't have it. You are a good King, Carlos Santi. Your own King."

Carlos smiled, and Eric turned to Eva. To his surprise, her eyes looked a little glassy.

"Are you crying?" he asked incredulously.

"No!" she said, punching him in the arm. "I was just starting to like you, Surface Boy."

He gave her a hug, and then she roughly wiped her eyes.

"Enjoy your demon world," she said sullenly.

"You two are welcome any time," Eric replied. "And until then, we will keep your secret."

"Thank you," Carlos said.

Eric squeezed through the opening, and Eva poked her head out behind him. She squinted, looking up at the sky in wonder. "Okay . . . that's just terrifying," she said. "Take care of yourself. Make some friends. Maybe even that pretty girl with the black hair. See you . . . Eric."

Eric laughed. "Finally."

She stepped back, and the boulder was rolled into place. From this side, it was simply an innocuous rock face tucked into the landscape, lined with brush and cacti and sandstone walls.

"Well," Eric said, turning to the sun, "let's go for a walk."

Twenty-Nine Hours Later

OFFICER BROWN WATCHED IN TREPIDATION AS the team descended into the opening. There were ten of them in all, each with climber's equipment, miner's caps, and first aid supplies. The all-clear had finally come from the geologists, and they had wasted no time.

The search needed to begin if they had any chance of finding survivors down there. Mr. Baker had woken up again and given them the exact location of the fall, so they at least had somewhere to start. He had been knocked unconscious and caught on the shore of a river, and had managed to crawl back up through the hole. He suspected the kids might have been dragged deeper underground. It was going to be a long search, and no one was very hopeful.

Officer Brown stood behind the yellow tape with the rest of the crowd. Cameras were flashing, reporters were talking, and the families were standing together, holding hands and watching. He saw Ms. Johnson standing alone, her arms folded over her chest, tears in her eyes. Mr. and Mrs. Rodrigues were close by, along with the Pikes, Lewskis, the Tams. All of the families were there today, waiting for news. He felt a nudge on his arm and saw his partner step up beside him.

"Well, at least we'll finally get some answers," she said.

"Yeah," Officer Brown said. "I'm not sure if that's good or bad yet."

"We did the best we could."

"We waited," he said grimly. "We did nothing, really, but wait."

"As we were ordered." She gave him a pat on the shoulder. "You should get some sleep."

He looked at her incredulously. "Now?"

"It's going to take them a while, Dan. Go home and see your family. You've barely been home since this started. I'll call you as soon as the team is back. You can come and help then."

"All right," he mumbled. "Thanks, Mel. Call me right away, no matter what."

"I will."

He forced a smile and started back to his car, thinking about the waiting families. He couldn't imagine what they were thinking. They all knew the odds. The rescue team wasn't expecting to find many survivors. Maybe none at all.

He sighed as he reached the cruiser, pulling open the car door. Mel was right. He needed to hug his daughter and his wife. He needed to stop staring at that cave and wishing for a miracle. Instead, he took a last look out at the horizon, wondering if the rescue team would be back before sundown. And then he saw a shape on the horizon. No. *Shapes.*

Fourteen Days Later

ERIC LIFTED HIS HEAD SLEEPILY AS MR. BAKER skipped into class. He figured Mr. Baker was probably the only person on Earth who *could* still skip with a knee-high cast and crutches. The bruises and cuts on Mr. Baker's face had mostly healed, leaving just a few puckered white scars that Mr. Baker affectionately referred to as his "explorer's initiation."

The rest of the class was back in school by now too; many had stayed home for several days nursing their injuries—mental and physical—but things were starting to feel normal. Eric had assumed most students would just stay home for the rest of the school year. Exams had been cancelled and summer break was only a few days away now, but it seemed everybody wanted to be back in the classroom. He certainly did. It was . . . comforting, somehow.

Eric had come back just a few days after their escape from the caves. He had been ready to return to school right away, but he also wanted to spend some time with his mom. She had barely left his side. He had even caught her sitting next to his bed one night when he woke up, as if she was afraid to let him out of her sight. But she had gone back to work now, and he'd insisted that she go out on a date with Frank. They were on their third date now, and Eric even kind of liked him.

He wasn't the first one back to class, though. Jordan had already told Mr. Baker what really happened in the caves and sworn him to secrecy, and Mr. Baker had quizzed them all relentlessly since. He seemed disappointed he'd missed all the excitement, but he was also endlessly fascinated by the story.

Mr. Baker spun on his heel at the front of the class, grinning. "Morning, class!"

"Morning, Mr. Baker," a few of the Keeners replied.

So far, everyone had kept their word. The official story was that they had fallen through a crack, washed into a lake, and managed to find their way back out again after a long but completely uneventful walk through the caves. Strangely, not one of them could remember *where* they had come out of the caves . . . just that it was somewhere in the desert. They blamed fatigue.

Eric glanced over at Silvia. Hanging out more with Silvia was the best thing that had come out of the field trip. Things had been crazy for a while: cameras, interviews, reporters waiting outside their homes. The group had taken on a lot of names in the newspapers, and finally *The Carlsbad Kids* seemed to stick. Through it all, Eric and Silvia had stayed close, having formed a strange bond in the caverns, even in the short time they actually spent together. When they were alone, they would wonder about Carlos and Eva and Jana and what was happening down there. And when they had nightmares about spiders or beetles, they would call each other. Even Ashley had begun to warm up to him. She seemed a lot less interested in acting cool since they'd come back. Silvia had joked that they'd all forgotten parts of themselves down there.

"How are we all today?" Mr. Baker asked. "I've been thinking about our field trip."

There were a few wary looks. Generally, they had tried to keep that topic out of the class in an attempt to get back to normalcy. Eric and Silvia exchanged a quick look across the room.

Mr. Baker smiled. "For one thing, in all the excitement, I forgot about the prize."

He went to his desk and fished something out of his bag. It was the copy of *Jim White's Own Story*. It was a bit ragged and curled, but besides that it had held together remarkably well.

"When I heard your stories, I was thinking about the amazing bravery and resourcefulness of my class. And the science! Fascinating that vegetation is growing down there. And yet I forgot to consider a more basic question: Who are they? How did they get there? And then, when I thought about the stories you had told me, especially Eric, I had a thought. And that shall be our skill-testing question," Mr. Baker said with a flourish. "Who are these people?"

The class fell silent. Eric stared at Mr. Baker for a moment, thinking of what Carlos had told him. That he was the fourth

King. Their great-grandfather had led his people down here 118 years ago.

Which was right around the time . . .

"Carlos's great-grandfather . . . ," Eric said in wonder. "Juarez Santi. He was the *Kid*."

"Very good, Eric!" Mr. Baker said. "My guess exactly. The book is yours! In it you will read about the Kid, who then disappeared from attention. I imagine he explored the caves well after Jim White had moved on, and then, three years later, he led people down into that great, undiscovered world and became the very first Midnight King."

Eric gratefully accepted the book, tucking it into his backpack.

"But that was the good news." Mr. Baker was no longer smiling. "We have a bit of a problem."

The class fell silent.

"The University of New Mexico has just announced that they will be launching a scientific expedition into the caves—down into the river the same way we went. The seismic activity has abated and they feel it's safe enough to do so. They are sending an entire team."

Eric felt his skin go cold. He looked at Silvia and saw the same concern on her face.

"When are they going?" Eric asked.

"In one month," he said, heading over to the calendar to draw a big X on one Monday in July. "I just read it in the newspaper this morning. A full expedition. They want to explore it all."

"But . . . they'll find Medianoche," Silvia said.

Mr. Baker nodded. "Most likely. Unless they're warned. It could be dangerous for the scientists too. Carlos's soldiers may decide to . . . remove the threat. It could be a big debacle."

"What do you mean by *unless they're warned?*" Tom asked carefully.

Eric sighed and leaned back in his chair. "It means we're going on another field trip."

Author's Note

When I was a kid, I wanted to run away. Not because my parents were mean or because I got grounded a lot, but because I wanted *adventure*. I loved adventure stories—especially ones where kids had to survive on their own. In my imaginary journeys, there were no adults allowed.

In fact, one of my all-time favorite books is the fabulous *My Side of the Mountain* by Jean Craighead George. All these years later, now that I am one of those grown-ups I was trying to escape from, it plays a part in my book. Funny how things work.

This book is my own humble addition to that tradition of nature adventure stories. It's a love letter to all the things that make those stories grand: courage, independence, and friendship. I have always found that adventure and fear have a curious habit of bringing people together. When people work together to survive, they discover that they are very much alike. They don't have time for cliques and bullies and gossip. I always loved that aspect of adventure stories, and it's why I chose to use three main characters. I wanted readers to experience the story from different perspectives: from one person wrapped in fear, another in their self-imposed isolation, and a third who couldn't move on from the past. In some ways, I have been every one of those people. I suspect the same is true for you. Sometimes it's good to remember that we are all just finding our way through the dark.

I knew this story was going to take place in a cave, and Carlsbad Caverns was the perfect setting. Though I have never been there personally, I am fascinated by its geology, its history, and, like all caves, its secrets. It truly is as magnificent as described in this book, and the story of Jim White and the Kid is also true (so are the four hundred thousand bats!). There has been speculation that Native Americans may have first discovered Carlsbad Caverns, and it seems likely, but Jim White was the first person to document his exploration. I researched the caverns extensively— and cave geology and zoology in general—through a bunch of different media, and a lot of that real-life information is in this book. These glow worms really do exist (including the long strands of mucus!), and Jordan's map is real. However, I decided to add a few details of my own: minor changes like giant spiders, a subterranean shark, and a lost civilization. In fact, I added a whole new world below the explored sections of the caverns. But who's to say that it isn't there? The world is still full of mystery.

If you have a chance, perhaps you can explore the wonders of Carlsbad Caverns yourself. Who knows? Maybe I will see you there.

And if you enjoyed exploring Carlsbad Caverns with our three heroes, there is plenty more to learn about this world-famous site. Check out these online resources:

National Park Service: https://www.nps.gov/cave/index.htm

National Geographic: http://video.nationalgeographic.com /video/us_carlsbadcaverns

Wikipedia: https://en.wikipedia.org/wiki/Carlsbad,_New_Mexico

Or watch the amazing *Planet Earth* episode "Caves" from the BBC (https://www.youtube.com/watch?v=3oUe8pusk3I).

And if you want to read the books mentioned in this story, they are:

My Side of the Mountain by Jean Craighead George (E.P. Dutton, 1959)

Jim White's Own Story by James Larkin White, as told to Frank Ernest Nicholson (1932)

Remember: Everyone has a story. What's yours?

Your friend in spelunking,
Wesley King

Did you like *A World Below*?
Turn the page to begin *OCDaniel*,
also by author Wesley King.

I first realized I was crazy on a Tuesday. I mean, I suspected it before, obviously, but I'd been hoping it was just a phase, like when I was three and I wanted to be a fire truck. But on that fateful October day she said hello after the last bell, and it was official—I was completely bonkers.

Tuesdays are usually my favorite day of the week. It's a weird day to like, but for me, a gangly, eccentric thirteen-year-old social oddity with only one real friend, it has some serious perks.

For one thing, we don't have football practice. Most kids probably like football practice, but when you're the backup kicker, you mostly just sit there and watch bigger, stronger kids run into each other and incur lifelong brain trauma. I know they're still studying that and all, but just talk to Dale Howard for a few minutes, and you can pretty much put a yellow warning label on the helmets.

Sometimes I get the team Gatorade—actually, I carefully arrange the cups into perfect geometric patterns to simplify drinking and reduce potential spillage—but that's the only fun part. Usually I just sit on the bench by myself and think about what would happen if aliens attacked the field and started laying radioactive eggs in the end zone. Or if flesh-eating monsters that only ate football players emerged from the ground and chased Coach Clemons. Or if we were attacked by an evil supervillain named Klarg who shot fire out of his eyeballs and was strangely vulnerable to orange Gatorade, which of course I had in huge supply. You get the idea.

The result is always the same: I save the world and never have to go to football practice again.

You might be asking why I go to football practice at all. The problem is that my dad; my older brother, Steve; and my best friend, Max, all love football and may stop talking to me altogether if I quit. I think I'm already pushing my luck with Max, so I just keep on playing. Or sitting on the bench, anyway.

I do some other stuff at practice too, but those are harder to explain. Like count the players and tie my shoes a lot and rearrange the cups after they're messed up. I think those are all fairly standard bored activities, at least for me. I do lots of things like that. Not really sure why. I spend most of my time hiding them from other people, so I can't exactly ask what's standard.

By the way, my name is Daniel Leigh. That's like "lee," not "lay." People get that wrong sometimes. I did say I was a thirteen-year-old social oddity, which is true. Actually I'm not sure what else to add. People say I'm smart, and I was in the Gifted Program when I was younger, until they got rid of it because it was a bit confusing to tell the other kids that some students were gifted and they weren't. Also I think they realized that if they continued the Gifted Program, us "gifted kids" would be separated our whole lives, but that happened anyway, so big deal.

I don't even know what being "gifted" means. I remember things easily and read novels every night, but that doesn't mean I'm smarter than Tom Dernt, who prefers to play football and is now superpopular. My teachers say I have a huge vocabulary and write way above my age level, but my brother told me to stop using fancy words or I'd never get a girlfriend. He has a girlfriend, so I have little choice but to heed his advice. I mean *take* his advice.

I also like to write. In fact, I am writing a book right now, though I don't tell anyone that—even my parents. I don't really want to share it, which will probably be an issue if I ever want to be published. It's called *The Last Kid on Earth.* It's an adventure story about a boy named Daniel.

Cryptic, I know. I have written the first page fifty-two times, and I am still not happy with it.

Oh, I also get distracted a lot and go on tangents. Which means I talk a lot about things you probably don't care about, so how is that smart? Let's get back to Tuesdays.

Geography is my last class of the day. It's one of my favorite subjects and rarely results in homework, since the long-suffering Mr. Keats usually just gives up on us and creates a work period so he can sit behind his desk and read the paper. There's no math that day either—another bonus, since I really stink at math. So no football, no homework, and, to make things better, Max usually comes over to play video games since his mom gets home late from work that night. Like I said, Tuesdays are the best. Well . . . usually. This Tuesday was not so great.

As usual, I was sitting next to Max, who was busy going on about our impending football game on Saturday morning against the Whitby Wildcats. He's on the team too, but he actually plays. Max is the tight end, which is way more important than the backup kicker—though, in fairness, so is every other position on the field. Of course, Max tends to forget that I don't even really like the sport and talks about it twenty times a day, but that's all right. We've been best friends since kindergarten, and he didn't ditch me when he got cool in the fifth grade and I didn't. In fact, being friends with him even keeps me on the distant fringe of the popular crowd, where I would never be otherwise. I'm like the guy the cool kids know but wouldn't actually call directly. That's better than being the guy who gets shoved into a locker, who I definitely would have been otherwise.

In any case, on that fateful day we were sitting in geography class and he was talking about football, and I was looking at Raya. Raya is a girl that we hang out with. Well, Max does. I hang out with Max, who hangs out with Raya. She's this cool girl who's really mature and way too pretty to look at the backup kicker of the Erie Hills Elephants. Yeah, not a great football name. We do this whole trunk thing before games. Never mind.

Back to Raya. She wears clothes that don't even make sense—cardigans and shawls and Technicolor stuff that aren't usually considered cool. I think. I wear T-shirts and hoodies that my mom gets at Walmart, so I'm not exactly a fashion expert, though I read plenty of articles online in case Raya ever asks me about it. For instance I know that men should really wear fitted dress shirts and pants with pleats if they want to look successful and attract women. I considered it for a while, but my brother told me that he would personally beat me up if I went to school with pleated khakis, so I just kept wearing hoodies. I also know that some Parisian fashion designers still use ivory, which I find upsetting because it means they are killing elephants for a necklace that could easily be made out of plastic. I like elephants.

They're clever, compassionate, and reportedly remember everything, though I can't confirm that. I'll try to stay focused.

Raya's hair is cut pretty short, and it always looks supertrendy and is usually died red or something. But I really don't care about any of that stuff. Okay . . . her eyes are really nice—they look like hot chocolate with marshmallows circling the mug, which is one of my favorite beverages. And she has a pretty smile that leans just a little to the right, revealing one of those pointy fang teeth. Those are just evolutionary remainders from our ancestors biting into sinewy raw meat and muscles, but for Raya the pointy fang teeth are perfect.

She is also smart and funny, and she has this little dimple that deepens on her right cheek when she laughs. How long had I been staring again?

"You're being a weirdo," Max said, nudging my arm.

"What?"

He sighed. "Case and point, Space Cadet."

Max calls me Space Cadet, by the way. I do this thing where my eyes glaze over and I stare at stuff and don't realize I'm doing it.

"You know, she has her flaws," Max said.

My infatuation with Raya Singh was well documented.

"No she doesn't," I said defensively.

"She does," Max insisted. "Most important, she doesn't like you."

"How do you know that?"

"A hunch."

I turned back to Raya and slumped, defeated. "You're probably right."

Max leaned in conspiratorially. "But you'll never know unless you ask."

I almost laughed. The class was kind of whispering to each other anyway, but a laugh might have been a bit too much and drawn unwanted attention. Mr. Keats was writing some stuff on the whiteboard, and we were supposed to be taking notes. I think a few people were, and I kind of wanted to, but Max always advised me that it was way cooler to not copy the notes. Worse for tests, though, I always noticed.

Max didn't always give me the best advice. He was like a cooler version of me. He was lean and muscular, with closely cropped black hair and piercing blue eyes. Girls liked him, though he seemed a bit leery of them, which he probably picked up from me. I was flat-out terrified of girls. Especially Raya.

"What should I ask her?" I said. "'Raya, do you like me?'"

He shrugged. "Sounds about right."

I looked at Max incredulously. "That was sarcasm."

"Oh. Well, I would just try it. What do you have to lose?"

"My dignity, pride, and self-respect." I paused. "Point taken."

I sighed and shifted my gaze to the whiteboard, where

Mr. Keats had finally stopped writing notes and was now looking out at the class in disapproval. If I had to describe him in fashion terms, it would be striped button-down shirts buttoned to the top and pleated khakis. Oh . . . my brother was right.

Written at the bottom of the board was:

Geography Test: THIS Friday, October 19th. STUDY, PLEASE.

Frowning, I picked up my pen and wrote the date down. At least I started to.

As I began writing "19th," my pen abruptly stopped on the page, halfway through the "1." Then it hit. I call them Zaps. They do different things sometimes, but there's a definite process that goes like this:

1. Bad thought
2. Terrible feeling or sensation like you just got attacked by a Dementor
3. Realization that you may die or go crazy or never be happy again if you don't do something fast

This time it went:

1. *There's something bad about that number.*

2. Tingling down neck and spine, stomach turns into overcooked Bavarian pretzel and hits shoes. *You will never be happy again for the rest of your life and you will think about it forever.*
3. Stop writing the number.

I don't know if that makes sense. It's like telling someone about a bad dream. They listen and they say "Oh, how terrible" but they don't really understand and they only half-care anyway because it wasn't real. And I think that's what people would say to me, but it is real. It's as real as anything. Think of the worst you have ever felt in your whole life—like if you got a bad flu or your dog died or you just got cut from a team you really wanted to be on— and imagine that happens when you take nine steps to the bathroom instead of ten. That's kind of what Zaps are like.

This wasn't a new thing. The Zaps happened, like, ten times a day—on some days, even more. I had no idea why, except for the logical reason that I was nuts. I didn't feel crazy, and I sincerely doubted that writing "19th" down on a certain line in my notebook was going to result in the end of the world. And yet I couldn't shake the feeling. I quickly scratched the number out.

"Why did you do that?" Max asked, glancing at me curiously.

I bit back a curse. I was extremely careful to hide the

Zaps, but I had lost focus for just a moment and had forgotten to check if Max was looking. My cheeks flushed.

"It was too messy," I said casually, avoiding his eyes. "Figured I'd miss the date."

Max snorted and went back to doodling. "Like you'd miss a test."

The rest of the class went by normally, with me stealing a few more looks at Raya.

Just before the day ended, the announcements crackled to life. The entire class jumped. Most had been either dozing off or talking quietly, as we had been given a work period to finish an assignment. I had already completed mine (which Max had copied), so we were talking about football. Well, Max was—I was just listening to him and thinking about how happy I was that there was no practice that night. Max was halfway through a story about a new route he had to run, when the principal's gruff voice cut in.

"Attention, classes. I have a quick announcement for the intermediates before the end of the day."

Principal Frost was not an overly happy guy. He looked like a cave troll and had a personality to match: dour and temperamental. Sometimes I wondered if he even went home after school, or if he just lived in his office surrounded by the piled bones of students who had gotten one too many detentions.

Principal Frost sounded even less thrilled than usual.

"As you may recall, our first annual Parent Council fund-raising dance will be happening two weeks from today," he said, sounding like the idea of a dance was making him nauseous. "Council has asked me to remind you to get your tickets now before they are sold out. Your teachers all have tickets available. Also, the noise in the hallways at the end of the day will not be tolerated. I will be walking around this afternoon handing out detentions. That is all. Oh, and clean your shoes off on the mats!"

With that, the announcement ended. The class instantly buzzed to life, with some of the girls looking excited and some of the guys making jokes or groaning. The principal had announced the dance at the beginning of the year, but I think everyone had kind of forgotten about it. Now my mind was racing. My eyes darted to Raya, who was of course looking completely oblivious to the news and listening distractedly to her friends. Was this my chance? Would anyone actually bring a date? I looked around. There certainly seemed to be a lot of whispering.

"This sounds lame," Max said.

"Agreed," I said, shifting a little and glancing at him. "But are you going to go?"

Max paused. "Probably."

Mr. Keats was shaking his head behind the desk, obviously realizing his assignment was long since forgotten.

The bell rang, and he just waved a hand. "Run along," he said. "Hand it in tomorrow."

Max and I quickly packed our stuff up and hurried out of the class. The conversations around us were still squarely focused on the dance. Taj, one of Max's football buddies, joined us, clapping Max on the shoulder and completely ignoring me. He did that a lot—probably because he was a foot taller and literally couldn't see me.

"You gonna ask someone to the dance?" Taj asked, grinning.

Max laughed. "I doubt it."

"No one is going to do that, right?" I chimed in.

"Why not?" Taj said. He was a big, burly kid who played linebacker. "I'm definitely going to. I don't want to be the kid sitting with you chumps while the rest of the boys are out there with the ladies."

"Ladies?" I asked, feeling my stomach flop over.

"An expression," Taj replied dryly. "Maxy, you need to ask someone. How about Clara?"

"She's a drama queen," Max said.

Taj winked. "And a hot one."

Max and Taj laughed while I hurried along beside them. So people *were* going to ask girls to the dance. Girls. Like Raya. Which meant I could theoretically ask her to go with me. I felt like I might vomit just thinking about it. Who was I kidding?

I was so preoccupied with the dance that I belatedly realized I was stepping on the tile cracks. There was no need to be reckless. I quickly adjusted my pace by three quarters so that my sneakers fell squarely on the dull white ceramic. I was a master of adjusting my stride so that no one would notice.

Up ahead a TA, Miss Lecky, was slowly walking down the hall, trailed by Sara Malvern. Sara was . . . different. She had gone to our school since preschool, but she was almost always taught separately from everyone else. She hadn't spoken once in all that time. Eight years, and not a word.

I still remembered the first day she joined a regular class. It was fifth grade, and when I walked in, she was sitting in the corner with a TA. Her eyes were on the board, and she didn't notice us walking in.

"Everyone say hi to Sara," my teacher, Mrs. Roberts, said before class.

We did, but Sara didn't even smile.

"Thank you," her TA said.

She didn't speak for weeks, of course. I saw her TA say things to her, but that was it. She just sat there and never responded.

It was November when she finally made a noise. She didn't talk. She screamed.

She looked off that day; flustered and sweaty and

fidgeting. She didn't usually fidget. I wasn't too far from her, so I saw it all. Her TA tried to calm her down, but it seemed to get worse. Finally I saw the TA try to grab her arm to calm her down. Sara screamed. The whole class jolted, and Mrs. Saunders dropped her chalk. Sara wrenched her hand away, pushed her desk over, and ran out into the hallway.

I never saw her in a regular class again.

I'm not sure if she could speak or if she had a learning disorder or what. Actually I had no idea what was wrong with her. Her big green eyes were always foggy and glazed over like she was looking at something far away. She didn't look at anyone or even seem to notice where she was. She just went through her day like a zombie, her mind elsewhere. She always wore a bracelet with a few little charms on it that jangled around as she walked, but I never saw what they were.

The other kids all called her Psycho Sara, but I had never seen her do anything crazy, besides that one time. She just seemed distracted. I could sympathize. Sometimes I felt pretty distracted myself.

Max, Taj, and I were just passing Sara when something unexpected happened.

She turned to me, her foggy eyes suddenly looking clear and sharp.

"Hello, Daniel," she said.